Sunny Dreams

Sunny Dreams

Alison Preston

Signature
EDITIONS

Cover design by Doowah Design.
Cover photo of Alison Preston by Tracey L. Sneesby.
This book was printed on Ancient Forest Friendly paper.
Printed and bound in Canada by Marquis Imprimeur.

Thanks to the Manitoba Arts Council for its generous support during the writing of this book.

Thanks to Bruce Gillespie, Karen Haughian, Betty McKush, John Preston, Jeanne Small and Chris Thompson.

We acknowledge the support of the Canada Council for the Arts and the Manitoba Arts Council for our publishing program.

Library and Archives Canada Cataloguing in Publication

Preston, Alison, 1949-
      Sunny dreams / Alison Preston.

ISBN 978-1-897109-20-5

      I. Title.

PS8581.R44S86 2007   C813'.54   C2007-905401-3

Signature Editions, P.O. Box 206, RPO Corydon
Winnipeg, Manitoba, R3M 3S7
www.signature-editions.com

for
Jean Adair Fraser Preston
1912-2001

PROLOGUE

1925

We went downtown in a Plaza taxi — my mother, Sunny, and me — to see our pediatrician. After our checkups with Dr. Maxwell we walked over to meet my dad for a ride home at the end of his working day. We brought the travelling carriage for Sunny because she couldn't walk yet.

Spring came early that year and the downtown sidewalks were dusty and dry. It was still March, but warm, unnaturally so. My mother and I wore summer dresses. We took sweaters with us, just in case, but they ended up in the carriage, bundled at Sunny's feet.

I loved the walk down Portage Avenue; there was so much to see. We passed the Rex Billiard Parlour with its no-gooders smoking in the doorway. I didn't know what it was about pool-playing men that made them no-gooders, but my mother said that's what they were and I believed her. We passed Mitchell Copp Jewellers where my dad bought my mum's wedding ring and where my future husband would buy mine if I had my way. We passed the United Cigar Store and Moore's Restaurant where my parents went for Boston cream pie after shows at the Capitol Theatre next door.

But best of all were the people.

"Don't stare, Violet," my mother hissed as I gaped open-mouthed at a woman with lipstick drawn up over her lips to make them appear bigger, I supposed. "And for goodness' sake close your mouth. You're going to swallow a fly one of these days."

We passed the man on his small wooden platform in front of the Clarendon Hotel.

"Why does that man have no legs?" I asked.

His platform had squeaky castors and sometimes he would roll along beside folk until they gave him a coin or two. My mum dropped a quarter in his hat today and said, "Shh!" to me.

My dad's office was in the Childs Building on Portage Avenue near Main Street. At twelve storeys it was the tallest building in Winnipeg and I bragged about that to whoever would listen. Funny the things I thought were important when I was six years old. My dad's office was on the seventh floor; I wished it were on the twelfth. A uniformed man named Harvey ran the elevator.

"Good afternoon, Mrs. Palmer," he said.

When my mum smiled at him he flushed beneath his cap. My mother had a way about her.

"Hi, kids." He clanged the outer door shut and then the brass inner gate. "Where to?" he asked.

I giggled. I was pretty sure he was kidding. He knew very well where we were going.

"Seven, please, Harvey," I said, to be on the safe side. After a moment's thought I added, "Sunny can't talk yet." I didn't want him to think her silence was rude. Then I said, "She's my sister." I also didn't want him to think she was a boy. She was too young to look like anything much and I had heard of boys called Sonny.

We were a little early. My dad wasn't finished work yet so we piled back into the elevator.

"Main floor, please, Harvey," I said. "We're going to have a snack while we wait for my dad." It was what I had been hoping for.

Harvey let us off after aligning the elevator floor perfectly with the floor in the lobby. It amazed me that he was always able to do that.

We went next door to Picardy's. The restaurant was crowded but we found a table in a corner behind a large potted fern. Mother settled Sunny. She didn't need much settling; she was sound asleep.

"You stay here with the baby, Violet, and I'll go up to the counter to choose our treats."

I was having none of that. I wanted to pick my own. She sighed and gave in to me. My mother wasn't much of a fighter.

There was chocolate cake and rhubarb pie and banana cream pudding and apricot tarts. I finally chose the chocolate cake. Mother added it to her bowl of pudding already on the tray. Sunny was too young for treats. Her needs were pretty basic, mostly involving milk.

I followed along behind my mother as she carried our tray back to the table. When it clattered to the ground every face in the room turned toward us. Moon-faced women and chisel-faced men and rosy-cheeked waitresses and busboys wearing hairnets. My mother scrabbled through the carriage and raced about the restaurant from table to table.

"Sunny!" she cried out. "My baby!"

The carriage looked the way it always did when Sunny wasn't in it. There was a soft dent in the pillow where her head had been. I touched it. It was warm.

My mum clutched at her throat where there was nothing but the flimsy collar of her summer dress.

"Help!" She didn't make a sound but we all saw the word leave her mouth.

A man in a dark suit took charge. He phoned the police from the restaurant phone on the wall next to the cash register. That frightened my mother even more. Surely it was too soon for those kinds of measures, she said. He tried to calm her and told everyone not to touch anything. Everything he said seemed to crank up my mum's terror a notch. I wondered if I should admit to having touched Sunny's pillow but I decided to keep it to myself.

"Maybe Will's got her," my mother said in an odd loud voice. "Maybe my husband slipped in and picked her up."

A waitress ran next door for my dad. We were well known at the restaurant: that nice lawyer's family.

My mother ran out to the street; the man who kept scaring her ran out too and women fussed over me. I stayed with the carriage, guarding it like I should have been doing all along. I placed my hands in the pockets of my dress to keep from touching anything and stared at my cake on the floor.

I don't think I considered that I would never see Sunny again or that my life would change drastically from that moment in time.

My dad hurried into the restaurant and over to me and the carriage. He seemed to know about the no-touching rule from the man in the suit or maybe he knew it on his own — my dad's quite smart. He picked me up and squeezed me, a little too tightly, but I didn't mind.

"Where's your mother?"

"I don't know."

The man in the dark suit and my mum came back in at that moment, followed by the police: two street patrollers at first and then others in regular clothes. The man in the suit let them take over from there.

"Thank you," my mum said.

My dad hurried over to her, not letting go of me, and they clung to each other.

"What happened, Anne?" my dad said.

I wriggled down.

"Oh, Will, I just don't know," said my mum through tears as she fell against him. "Our baby's gone."

No one knew anything. No one was very sure of having seen anything. There were one or two vague recollections of a tall man in a tan suit near the potted fern, but nothing concrete.

The police were trying to keep people clear of the area. I heard them talk about footprints and fingerprints. The floor in Picardy's was so clean I could have eaten my chocolate cake off of it, but one young policeman who looked familiar to me was down on his hands and knees looking for something on the floor that would help us to find my sister. It was called a clue. I didn't know what a clue was yet, but I figured it must be pretty small if he had to look for it that closely. I didn't hold out much hope for him.

My mum stood by the carriage again, staring into it. I moved to be beside her and I heard little animal sounds coming from her throat. A lady in a pink hat tried to get her to sit down but she wouldn't or couldn't.

Dad was on the phone by the cash register. He knew people, my dad. He would know the right person to call to get Sunny back in her carriage where she belonged. But when I walked over to listen, I realized that it was just Mr. Larkin on the line, our neighbour and my dad's good friend. Dad had called him to come with his car and take my mum and me home. Then he phoned the chief constable, who was also his friend.

The familiar-looking policeman, the one who had been looking for a clue, came over to speak to my dad. He held out his hand.

"Ennis Foote, Mr. Palmer. I live in your neighbourhood. I believe our kids know each other." He nodded at me.

"Of course," said my dad and took Mr. Foote's hand. "Thanks for being here."

"I just want you to know, sir, that we'll find your baby. I promise you that."

"Thank you…Ennis, is it?"

I could feel my dad's impatience. It was time to get moving and that's just what the police were doing — calling in more officers and hitting the streets. They were already out on Portage Avenue, Main Street, Albert Street and Notre Dame. The Childs Building where my dad worked was being searched from top to bottom. More calls were made to the bus depot, the train stations and to the provincial police.

At six years old I was too young to understand the intricacies of all that was going on around me but I'll never forget the smell of my mother's fear. On normal days she smelled like flowery soap with powder on top, like icing. But on this day she smelled like a skunk — a damp wrung-out skunk. I'd seen skunks and I'd smelled them and that was exactly what it was like. And her dress was black and white.

My dad was a stranger — his talk was of rifles and busting heads. I'd never heard words like that come out of him before and haven't since.

Mr. Larkin came and my dad tried to get my mum and me into the back seat of his car. My mum looked at him as though he had asked her to please lick the sidewalk with its felty covering of dust. Policemen were examining that dust.

"What good will it do for me to go home?" she asked.

"There are hundreds of men looking, Anne," Dad said. "It only makes sense for you to take Violet home and wait there for us to find her."

"Was her blanket gone?" my mother asked.

I noticed that her face was greasy looking. I'd never seen my mum with a greasy face before and it scared me more than anything that had happened so far. She reminded me of the lipstick lady.

"What?" said my dad.

"Was her blanket gone from the carriage?"

"I don't know."

"Please check."

Dad went back inside Picardy's and came out again carrying my sweater over his arm, but not my mum's. "Her blanket is gone," he said. "They took her blanket."

My mum didn't ask about her sweater so I didn't mention it either. I guessed that whoever took Sunny and her blanket took my mother's sweater as well.

Mr. Larkin and my dad finally succeeded in getting us into the back seat of the automobile. My dad kissed us both and Mr. Larkin drove us home.

His wife was waiting at our house. She came in with us and made tea and sandwiches. No one ate anything.

"Maybe someone just borrowed Sunny," I said to no one in particular.

"That's a nice thought, Violet, dear," said Mrs. Larkin.

"I'm going back downtown," said Mr. Larkin. "Will you be all right?"

His wife nodded and my mum and I were silent.

Mrs. Larkin helped my mum to change into clean clothes. She wouldn't have a bath but she accepted a cool washrag for her face.

No one outwardly blamed me, but I knew it was my fault. I should have stayed with Sunny and let my mother pick out our treats on her own. I would have liked whatever she brought me. But I wanted to see: the looking and choosing part was almost as good to me as the eating. I thought about my chocolate cake lying in a gooey mess on the floor in Picardy's. At the time, in the moments before I noticed my mum smelling like a skunk, I clearly remember mourning my chocolate cake more than my baby sister.

"She's such a good baby," my mother said now.

And I'm such a bad child, I thought.

"She never cries," Mother said.

I often did. It went without saying.

"She has a lovely disposition, our Sunny."

"What's a disposition?" I asked, glad my mum was talking, even if it was about how great Sunny was compared to me.

"Temperament," my mum answered. "She has a lovely temperament."

She stuck her slender arms into the fresh white blouse that Mrs. Larkin found in her bedroom closet.

"What's a temperament?" I asked, knowing I should be quiet.

Mrs. Larkin looked scared but my mum didn't seem to hear me.

"That's why I called her Sunny," she said. "I'll tell you a secret, shall I?"

A strange small smile curled her lips as she looked at neither of us and I felt very afraid. That smile was new to me.

"Yes," said Mrs. Larkin as she buttoned my mother's blouse. "Please tell us."

"Sunny's real name is Mary. That's the name on her birth certificate. We named her for Will's maternal grandmother. But it never suited her. I started calling her Sunny and Will did too."

The phone rang downstairs. My mum raced to answer it and Mrs. Larkin and I followed more slowly. It was my dad. He had nothing to report. He was just checking in. How were we? Fine, my mum said.

I think her explanation about Sunny's name contained the most sentences she uttered on any one day after Sunny's disappearance. My mother didn't talk a lot at the best of times. I remember thinking that an amazing number of words were coming out of her mouth under the circumstances. I don't think I was listening so much as just watching.

She sat in the kitchen and waited. She sat very straight. Mrs. Larkin didn't know what to do or say and neither did I.

"Thank God it's spring," she said at one point.

My mother didn't answer.

Mrs. Larkin stood up to put the kettle on for more unwanted tea.

The search party looked all day and all night. My dad came home and went out again and came home and went out again. He phoned my Aunt Helen and asked her to come stay with us. She was in Winnipeg, anyway, on a short vacation from her home in the Queen Charlotte Islands. She was staying downtown with a nurse friend who lived in an apartment on Carlton Street. The friend's name was Grace Box and she and Aunt Helen had been in the war together. They had nursed injured soldiers at Vimy Ridge and Passchendaele. My aunt had risen to the rank of Major.

My dad must have felt guilty leaving us on our own and Mrs. Larkin wasn't someone we knew well. Mr. Larkin was the good friend and he was out searching with my dad.

Aunt Helen was better than Mrs. Larkin as our companion. She hugged me a lot and made us food that was easy to swallow, like tapioca pudding and macaroni.

The first night I don't think my mother went to bed at all. I heard her going into Sunny's room and roaming around the house. I slept some. Now and then, when I heard the screen door slam, I went to my window and saw her sitting at the picnic table in the back yard. Helen tried to keep her company without being intrusive. I heard their soft murmurs from downstairs but mostly it was quiet.

I still think of that first night sometimes, even now, when I lie awake. The darkness is short-lived in Winnipeg in the summer but that night seemed to last forever. Finally the sky began to lighten and my dad came home again and Helen began to putter in the kitchen. My mum sat stiffly at the dining room table. I wondered if Sunny was dead.

The paper that morning ran the headline: CITY LAWYER'S BABY SNATCHED. My dad and Helen tried to hide it from my mum but she was too fast for them.

"So, it's official," she said to my dad. "Our baby is gone."

Posters were made with Sunny's description: ten months old, sixteen pounds, blonde curly hair, pale blue eyes, long lashes, fair complexion, good-natured, wearing pale yellow sleepers.

My mum objected to the inclusion of the fact that the baby was wearing sleepers because she thought it would reflect badly on her as a mother.

"What kind of mother takes her baby downtown in sleepers?" she asked my dad.

"A beautiful and good mother," he answered and her sore red eyes filled again with tears.

The police told my parents to expect a "ran some" note. I didn't know what that was but I waited for it along with everyone else. I knew it meant that Sunny would come home if she wasn't dead and that my life would return to the way it was.

No note came.

My dad offered a reward to anyone with anything that could help lead us to Sunny. I don't remember how much he offered but it was a lot.

The police questioned all the known criminals in Winnipeg, even the Willis twins who lived in our neighbourhood and were well-known to us. It seemed far-fetched to me that those two fourteen-year-old boys, even in and out of reform school as they were, could have anything to do with a man in a tan suit and an act so cunning. I knew them. They knew me and my mum and even Sunny from our walks through the streets with the carriage. My mum tried to avoid them but sometimes couldn't manage it.

"Hi, lady," they said. "Hi, girl."

They didn't say hello to Sunny but that would have been because they knew she was too young for it to be of any benefit.

My mum warned me that they were bad.

"Bad how?" I asked.

"They steal things from people and once they attacked an elderly man in his own home."

"Why?" I asked.

"I don't know," said my mum, "but it was terrible. They hurt him so badly he had to go to the hospital."

"That's worse than stealing," I said.

"Yes."

We heard that the Willis twins had joined in the search for Sunny. The reward money would have been impossible for them to ignore.

"I don't want them to be the ones to find her," said my mum.

"They wouldn't hurt her," said my dad. "And it's unlikely they'll find her."

"What do you mean?" my mother cried.

"Oh, Anne, I don't mean anything," sighed my dad. "I just meant of all the people in the world looking for Sunny it would be unlikely if the Willis boys were the ones to find her. Someone will find her, just not them."

And my mum fell asleep sitting up.

In those first days my mother became irritated if anyone mentioned something day-to-day like it looked like rain, or how about a soft-boiled egg? or would she like a blouse pressed?

"Of course not," she would snap and shake her head back and forth quickly, over and over.

Then she would go quiet again.

I remember sitting next to her on the couch trying to rest up against her rigid body.

"Could you please leave me now, Violet?" she said. "Run along and sit somewhere else."

At first I felt like she sometimes wished it were me that was stolen. Gradually I came to know that she always felt that way. I wasn't the child left behind, to cherish. I was a living presence that should have been an absence.

My dad didn't make me feel that way, so I began to stay away from my mother and turn towards him and Aunt Helen. My aunt would lie down with me sometimes at night till I went to sleep. I loved it when she did that because I knew then if the kidnappers came for me that she wouldn't let them take me away. She would fight them off. Aunt Helen was a lovely strong wall of fragrant protection.

Police departments across Canada aided in the search. There was talk of shady adoption outfits operating out of the east, babies bought and sold for large sums.

And there were rumours: a young woman from a Métis shantytown on the south side of the city was seen carrying a small crying bundle into the camp; a baby in yellow sleepers was spotted alone and asleep on the Transcona bus.

There were crank calls: we have your baby; we've seen your baby; we roasted and ate your baby. Someone even held a crying infant up to a phone so my mum could hear its wails. And there were crank letters: our neighbours have your baby; a wolf took your baby; your baby is a witch, you're better off without her. All calls and letters were followed up by the police and discarded as groundless.

The sincere calls were almost as hard to take, well-meaning women with too little in their lives to keep them from reaching out to strangers about something that was none of their business. My mum stopped answering the phone and Aunt Helen dispatched the callers with a no-nonsense brusqueness. They never called twice after dealing with Helen.

There were even gawkers. Whole families would come to look at the house where the kidnapped baby had lived. My dad called the police whenever that happened and they were driven away, hopefully in shame. For a time a policeman was stationed outside our house to keep those sorts of people away.

"It's unconscionable," said Aunt Helen.

"Yes!" I said. The word sounded to me like it fit the occasion perfectly.

My dad looked like an older man now, with lines running up and down his face. The lines didn't suit him.

"Go to sleep, Daddy," I said on some days when the way that he looked upset me.

"Listen to your daughter," said Aunt Helen. "You look a fright, Will."

And he would lie down on the couch and close his eyes but I don't think his sleeps were ever very deep.

Aunt Helen had taken an indefinite leave of absence from her nursing job out west but her employers wanted her back. That scared me more than anything, more than the kidnappers coming for me. I prayed to God and Jesus and the Holy Ghost that she would never leave. I wasn't sure who or what the Holy Ghost was but I wanted to cover all the bases. Aunt Helen caught me once, on my knees beside my bed. She was very kind: she thought I was praying for my sister to come home.

Then one morning she left in her brisk and smiling way. For me it was the worst thing that could happen: worse than Sunny never coming home, worse than my mum dying. My dad and I saw her off at the train station.

"Don't go," I said quietly as she crouched to kiss me goodbye.

She touched my cheek and boarded the train.

"Bo-oard!" shouted the conductor and we watched through the windows as Helen found her seat and settled in.

She waved at us and tried to be gay, but I knew her smile was an act, just for me. Her parting gift.

I practised her pretend smile on the ride home from the station.

"What are you doing, Violet?" my dad asked nervously as he manoeuvred the car over the bumpy roads.

"Nothing," I said.

I practised some more in front of my bedroom mirror but I looked nothing like Helen and I wasn't going to be able to comfort myself with any version of her pasted-on going-away smile.

My mother took to calling Sunny "Mary" and referring to her in the past tense as if she were dead, as if there were no hope. My dad did neither of those things but he didn't fight with Mother about it. He was afraid of her. At least, that's the way it seemed to me — afraid of what she was turning into. His grief was different from hers. It was grief, where my mum's was something else that didn't have a name that I knew of. I think that was because she was aware that if she had behaved just a little differently that day, if she had sat down at the table and waited for a waitress to come, or if she had ordered me to stay with Sunny while she picked out our treats, or if we had just waited up in my dad's office for him, then it would never have happened. It was down to her. Just like I believed it was down to me.

She didn't sleep normally anymore. Sometimes she nodded off for hours fully dressed in a chair. It seemed she was always fully dressed. And she lost so much weight her bones stuck out; she was all pointy edges. Her beautiful thick brown hair turned dull; some of it turned white and a lot of it fell out. She became a thin-haired person.

My mother seldom left the house. Sometimes she would sit in the backyard while I played, but she wouldn't play with me. I was pretty much left to my own devices.

We had a milkman and a bread man and an egg man who delivered their goods right to our back door. Meals were makeshift affairs, with my dad going to the fridge and bringing an assortment of items to the kitchen table: pickles, cheese, canned salmon, soda crackers. He did it for me and I wished he wouldn't. I would have been happier starving along with them.

"Her little feet get cold," my mother said one day. And she wouldn't let it go. "Will, tell someone to tell them to keep Mary's feet warm."

My dad didn't know what to do. Finally he phoned his friend, the chief constable, and told him that Sunny's feet sometimes got cold. The chief phoned his friend, the editor of one of the daily papers, who saw to it that a plea was sent out to the captors to look after the baby's feet. The other paper followed suit.

The search went on for months, but my sister wasn't found. I thought it was time my mother got back to her remaining child, me. I tried my best to be good.

In late July the police chief came to our house and brought Patrolman Ennis Foote with him. My dad was at home, thank goodness. He tried to get my mum to come downstairs but she wouldn't. I came, though, and the two men were very nice to me. I realized now that Mr. Foote was Fraser Foote's dad. Fraser was a boy in my Sunday school class who I liked a lot.

The chief told us that they weren't by any means closing the case but that they did have to let up a little on the search. They simply didn't have the manpower.

So they weren't shutting it down but everyone knew that keeping it open was just for show.

On August 16th, that summer of 1925, the first cool day announcing the coming of fall, my mother took Dad's Ford and drove it at full speed into the brick and limestone wall of the Nutty Club building downtown. Her neck broke and her skull smashed and it was over for her. I guess the idea of dragging herself through the winter ahead without Sunny was more than she could face.

There was an effort to protect me from this, from the way it happened, but I managed to bust through that protection and I don't think I missed much.

"What about us?" I remember asking my dad. He held me close and buried his face in my hair. I felt his warm tears on my scalp.

When my mother died Aunt Helen came back to us from her home in the Queen Charlottes. She stayed for a few weeks and then went home again. My dad cooked a bit now: pork and beans, bacon and eggs, and lots of Cream of Wheat. We also ate toasted tomato sandwiches till they came out of our ears. Then, after a few more weeks, Helen returned to us and stayed.

Dad worried about her leaving a whole life behind: her job, good friends, her small rented house. But Helen stressed to him that her situation out west was never meant to be permanent, that one of the reasons she'd become a nurse was because she'd liked the idea of pulling up stakes from time to time. She could find a job anywhere in the world.

"I'm sure you could come up with a far more exotic location than Winnipeg," argued my dad.

"Exotic!" Helen argued back. "After Vimy Ridge, Winnipeg is plenty exotic for me."

She had never married. When I asked my dad about that he told me that she'd been in love with a soldier once, back in 1917. She'd cared for him at a casualty clearing station near the front lines. Then she'd met up with him again in a hospital on the coast of France where she was stationed for a time that same year. Artillery shrapnel had taken one of his legs and bayonet lacerations went so deep that he didn't stand a chance. I pictured him oozing and bleeding beneath his thin hospital blanket.

"Helen was with him when he died," said my dad.

"He was lucky," I said.

"Lucky?"

"To have Helen looking after him while he was dying."

I think Dad had missed her when she was gone almost as much as I had. When she came back to stay, his newly hunched shoulders straightened slightly and he no longer forgot to pick up his feet when he walked or wore his bedroom slippers outside in the yard. That new habit of his had worried me terribly. It seemed a very slovenly thing for my dad to do.

We could have made it, the two of us, but it was much better having Helen around. Her bustling female presence went a long way in filling up the gaping chasm that my mother had left behind.

The baby's absence made a hole too, and I felt it, but on an entirely different plane. I'd had so little time to grow attached to Sunny and that had been in a kind of audience capacity. She was like a little moving picture that blew spit bubbles and raised the odd stink. She was too young for me to play with. The criminals stole her from us when I was six and Sunny hadn't yet celebrated her first birthday.

It must have been during those terrible months in the spring and summer of '25 that I started my lifelong habit of conjuring up in my mind The Worst That Could Happen. In the beginning, all my imaginings featured Sunny. I turned her into a cripple before she even arrived at her new home: she lost the use of her arms and legs. To me, that was the worst thing on the planet Earth that could befall anyone, worse even than crashing head first into the Nutty Club. At least if you did that you wouldn't be around to realize what had happened to you.

Our family's primary claim to fame before that summer was that my dad's dad, Grandpa Palmer, had gone down with the *Titanic*. I knew it, but didn't feel it, so it was easy to talk about. Even my dad didn't mind when I brought it up on occasion. But Sunny's kidnapping and my mother's death never took on enough distance for us to be able to talk about them comfortably even among ourselves.

Every year on the anniversary of Sunny's disappearance my dad put an ad in all the major papers across Canada. Each time he worded it a little differently, according to how old she got to be and how much he imagined her to have grown. He never got a serious answer. There are an awful lot of cranks out there in the world.

CHAPTER 1

Eleven Years Later

My family had been out of quarantine for a fortnight when I finally persuaded Fraser to go with me to see the boys.

At first, Johnny Lee was reluctant to talk to us.

"I thought it was just a pile of thistles," he said at last.

So the part about the Russian thistles was true.

We sat around the dining room table at a big house in Riverview: Johnny Lee, Fraser Foote, and I. We had been lucky enough to catch Johnny when his mother wasn't home.

The boy started to cry. I was sorry for putting him through this, but not sorry enough to stop.

"It must have been hard for you," I said.

"Leave my brother alone."

We hadn't noticed a little girl standing in the doorway to the kitchen.

"Go play in the backyard," Johnny said roughly.

"No."

"Go play in the backyard, Muriel, or I'll tell Mum you snuck cookies."

"I didn't sneak," Muriel said quietly as she backed away from us through the kitchen. "You snuck." The screen door closed behind her.

"That's my sister," Johnny said. "She's five."

A familiar sad worm wiggled inside my chest. Seven years ago our Sunny would have been five and I'd missed it.

"Does Muriel know about what you found?" I asked Johnny.

"I don't know," he said. "Probably. She knows something bad happened."

In late August of 1936 two eleven-year-old boys from Riverview became famous because of something that they found by the railway tracks. Johnny Lee was one of those boys and the other one was Artie Eccles. Their names weren't in the paper but news like that travels fast and their identities were bandied about soon enough. Fraser pestered his dad into confirming the names for us. His dad was a cop.

The phone book told us where we could find the boys. Riverview is on the other side of the Red River from the Norwood Flats where Fraser and I lived. It was a part of town that we mostly saw from across a muddy expanse of water. People just like us lived there, I'm sure, but they had always seemed exotic to me simply because they were as tiny as toy soldiers and they lived west of the Red. It was more like south-southwest at that bend in the river but there were too many curves to label them all with particularity. West held an allure for me probably because everything I knew best was east of the waterway. We had the motorboat launch and the Rowing Club and even a golf course on our side, but somehow Riverview's westness beat out all three, in my mind.

On a larger scale, reports of drought and wind and misery from the western provinces seemed to me more fascinating than the tales of grief from back east. And west coast salmon was far more enticing than the cod that bullied its way in from the east. No one liked that salty cod.

It was a Saturday afternoon in September when Fraser and I trudged through St. Vital, across the Elm Park Bridge to Jubilee Avenue. I knew there was a shorter way, but Fraser insisted on being the navigator and I was so grateful to him for coming with me that I didn't argue.

The sun slanted down on us from a deep blue sky fancied up with puffy white clouds. The days as we moved into autumn had become oddly clear of dust and no wind disturbed the stillness of the day. It was hot for that time of year, but hot was nothing new;

we were old hands at hot. The leaves were turning and they hung motionless from the trees that were too young to provide much shade — just a dappling here and there.

By the time we got to Artie Eccles' house on Balfour Avenue, I had a blister on one heel and a blouse soaked with sweat. And I had managed to kick my right anklebone with my left penny loafer so many times that I was bleeding through my thin white sock. I often did that.

Mrs. Eccles wouldn't let us speak to her son. She kept pushing him behind her as though to protect him from a couple of wild boars. He wanted to talk — I could tell — but she wouldn't hear of it. If she'd had a stick she would have beaten us off with it.

Johnny Lee lived on Morley Avenue, just one street away from the St. Mary's Cemetery. There were no adults at home there. His mother was at work, he'd said. No mention of a dad. The snag was he didn't want to talk about it.

"I'd rather not," he said, peering at us from behind the big front door.

"The man was my friend," I said.

His shoulders hunched up closer to his ears and he stared at the space between us.

I was sick with thirst. We stood there for another moment and then I asked for a glass of water.

He let us in then and led us to the dining room. He brought water in a pitcher and three glass tumblers. Fraser and I drank greedily.

Johnny was blubbing into his sleeve now and Fraser looked uncomfortable; he wasn't as sure as I was that this whole thing was a good idea.

"We sometimes put metal slugs on the tracks when a train's coming to see how flat they get," Johnny said. "We always play down by the tracks, building fires and roasting stuff."

The tears kept falling, but Johnny's voice was steady and I no longer felt like I was forcing him into anything. He wanted to talk. Maybe he hadn't talked enough. Maybe his mum didn't want to hear it.

"Nothing horrible ever happened to us before," he said. "It was always fun down there, till now."

"It'll be fun again one day," I said, not sure if it was a lie.

He looked at me as though I had no reasoning powers. I worried my bloody ankle with my left foot and regretted my words. I chose not to worsen the situation by speaking further. Finally, he went on.

"We each had a wiener," he said. "And a bun. We were gonna roast them. We were walking on the wooden slats between the rails. No trains were coming."

His shoulders hunched again when he said this and he looked like he expected someone to yell at him for playing on the tracks. It was the kind of thing boys got yelled at for.

Fraser reached out and put a hand on his shoulder. "It's okay, Johnny," he said.

The tears had stopped. They left their salty tracks on his smooth tanned face.

"I threw my wiener away," the boy continued. "I couldn't eat it after what we saw."

Again, that guilty look. It was unheard of for a thinking being to throw away any morsel of food in those hard years. And again, Fraser said, "That's okay."

"What did you see, Johnny?" My voice came out barely above a whisper.

"At first I thought it was just a pile of thistles by the tracks. But Artie thought it looked weird with all those flies. I did too. There were so many flies."

It was hot in the dining room. We had finished the water. When Johnny paused again Fraser picked up the pitcher and went to the kitchen to fill it from the tap.

Johnny looked at the tabletop and waited for Fraser to return. What he told us next hadn't been in the newspaper. We knew about it by now, but not from the paper, which hadn't told us much at all.

"There was no head," he said, his eyes on mine now, his lips trembling slightly.

"Most of the flies were at the head end."

Head end. It was an odd phrase, unlike any that we were used to hearing.

"The end where the head had been," said Johnny.

"Yes," Fraser and I said together.

"His head had been on the rail when a train went by. That's what the firemen said." Johnny's tears started up again.

"It was flattened to nothing. We knew it had been there because of the flies. They made a great buzzing pile by the neck hole."

Neck hole.

"The hole where…"

"Yes."

"Other insects too, ants, and ones I didn't even know what they were — new ones."

Fraser handed Johnny his damp handkerchief.

The trains that we heard from across the river in Norwood were the ones that travelled those rails where the boys played. They headed to and from the CNR Station on Main Street. They were in the background of our lives most days and nights, and usually I didn't notice them. But sometimes if I lay awake in the dark hours I imagined that I was a woman on a train, travelling alone with an expensive leather bag and a modern hairdo. I saw myself in fashionable trousers, tossing out witticisms to anyone who spoke to me, mostly porters and conductors, but sometimes a rich businessman who wanted me for his mistress. They all admired me no end.

I allowed myself now to picture a well-loved head being crushed to nothing.

Death by passing trains certainly wasn't unheard of in those days, but mostly it was accidental — too much hooch — or in some cases a messy suicide.

But not this time. This was murder. His naked body had been covered with tar and then plastered with Russian thistles: tarred and thistled. That part had been printed in the paper.

CHAPTER 2

Three Months Earlier

In the spring of 1936, Bruno Richard Hauptmann, whether rightly or wrongly, was cooked in an electric chair for the murder of the Lindbergh baby. Although it happened a long way away in another country, the kidnapping of Charles Lindbergh Jr. and the trial of his abductor was an event that resonated endlessly within the walls of our well-kept home. We had followed the news with heavy hearts.

Aunt Helen was still with us after all these years. Mostly she looked after us, but occasionally she took a private nursing job if someone asked for her in particular.

"Thank goodness that's over," she had said when we heard about Hauptmann on the radio news.

I wasn't so sure. Now whose job was it to kill the executioner? What about the ten commandments? What about, Thou shalt not kill? I was very back and forth about religion in those days, but certain parts of the bible were pretty hard to argue with.

My dad said nothing.

Our Sunny had never come home and, unlike the Lindberghs, we never received a ransom note or any communication at all from her kidnappers.

Over the years I came to believe that criminals were raising her, that her underwear was filthy and her hair full of knots all through her childhood. Her teeth would be rotting and crumbling in her mouth. I pictured her in New York City, a place so big that she would go unnoticed as someone who didn't belong.

I had stopped a long time ago trying to discuss these sorts of things with my dad or Aunt Helen. Neither of them wanted to speculate about Sunny. I became convinced that they thought she was dead or at least that they found it easiest to believe that was so.

That June I graduated from grade eleven at Norwood Collegiate. I scored a fifty R in mathematics. The R stood for reread, which I requested after receiving a failure, at forty-eight per cent. My teacher, Mr. Abernethy, was an easygoing man. There couldn't have been an extra two marks in there anywhere; maths isn't that kind of subject. I applied for the reread in the hopes that he would take pity on me, and he did.

In those days you could enter college straight out of grade eleven and that was my plan. I imagined that once I was out of high school I would start performing better, but I still didn't have any idea what I wanted to be — for sure nothing that involved maths or chemistry — those were my worst subjects. Any ambitions remained unclear to me, hidden under a woolly fog of confusion.

My dad was no help. His vision of my future was marriage to an up-and-coming prince of a man and many strong-limbed children for him to bounce on his knee. And he wouldn't leave it alone.

Finally, one day, I raised my voice to him and said, "I don't want to get married and have kids and lose one of them and become so sad that I drive myself into a stone wall. I don't want to depend on a husband and children to keep me alive and kicking."

He grew quiet and I apologized and he never mentioned it again and I sometimes wished he would.

Instead he decided to try and encourage me in different ways but I don't think his heart was in it. He would call out ideas from time to time.

"How about a nurse, like your Aunt Helen?"

"I don't think so, Dad," I said, "but thanks for the suggestion."

There was no way, even in the farthest reaches of my imagination, that I could picture myself mopping up the errant bodily fluids of the sick and jabbing needles into their withered rear ends. I knew there was more to it than that. It was rewarding work, the way Aunt Helen described it, but definitely not for me.

That summer I worked for Eaton's mail order. In the winter, I had worked there on Saturday mornings, but when my final exams were over, I began a three-day-a-week schedule: Monday, Tuesday, and Friday. People said I was lucky to get the job. Others, like Mrs. Walker, Gwen's mum, said I shouldn't have taken it away from someone who really needed it. Gwen was my best friend and she suggested that I ignore her mother, which I tried to do. But she could really get to me.

I lied to get the job, pretended that I would be staying on in the fall. They didn't want to train me just to have me up and quit. I felt a small amount of guilt about lying and about leaving them in the lurch come fall, but not too much.

We were well-to-do, even during the Depression when so many people were struggling. Besides my dad having a well-paying job there was wealth from my mother's side, from her father, who had been an architect and builder. My mum had been an only child and both my maternal grandparents had died soon after I was born — Grandpa from a massive stroke, Grandma from something that no one wanted to talk to me about. I knew she had bled to death but I didn't know from where.

"Was it in childbirth?" I had asked more than once, figuring that would be a good way of identifying the orifice without uttering any unpleasant words.

"No," was all I got from either Helen or my dad. I guess they were done talking about death.

My dad didn't care if I had a summer job — he would have been fine with my staying around home — but I wanted to buy clothes and shoes and makeup and magazines without asking him for money all the time. He was fairly generous, but he did question some of my purchases, especially if I bought two of something, like two lipsticks in different shades.

"Why do you need two?" he asked.

"Because on different days I feel like wearing different colours," I said.

"I don't think your mother ever had more than one lipstick on the go at the same time." He measured everything womanly by the way my mum had done it.

And look where she ended up, I thought. But what I said was, "So?"

"Yes, well," he said.

And there it would end.

I could barely remember my mother by now. She was something inside me that caused my jaw to clench and that curled my hands into fists. And she was a face in old photographs that Dad insisted on keeping around. They lost all meaning for me. They became less familiar than the cartoons in the funny papers. Blondie at least had bubbles filled with words coming out of her mouth and a friend named Tootsie Woodley. I didn't know if my mother had had any friends; I couldn't remember any, but that meant nothing. And it wasn't something I felt I could ask my dad.

Sometimes I would catch him crying when he didn't know I was around. Once I found him crying in my mum's closet where her clothes still hung and that made me mad. I pretended that it scared me and told Aunt Helen about it: fear seemed more acceptable than anger. She made my dad pack up the clothes and give them away to the church.

My position at Eaton's mail order was in the complaint department. I answered letters and tried to fix people's problems, like Ruth Block's, which landed in my tray on a June morning:

Hamiota, Manitoba
June 10, 1936

Dear Eaton's,

I received the size 14 blouse that I ordered but it doesn't fit me. It's snug under the arms and that won't do. Although I've never taken a size 16 before I would like to order one at this time. Please send it soon.

Yours truly,
Ruth Block

P.S. I'll hang on to the size 14 until I receive the substitute. Thanks.
RB

I sighed as I fed two new pieces of paper separated by a carbon sheet into my typewriter. It was one of a long run of mornings when my clothes stuck to me like paste and the Eaton's hosiery regulation seemed downright cruel. I explained to Ruth Block that she had to return the snug blouse before we could send her a new one. And that if she'd had the sense to do that in the first place she would have her size 16 a darned sight sooner. I didn't type in this last part, just thought it and mentioned it out loud to Mary Cartwright, the girl who sat at the desk beside me, doing the same job I did.

Mary had the same name as my little sister but I didn't often think of that because I still thought of my sister as Sunny. I often wondered what the criminals called her. For sure they would have changed her name.

When I told Mary about Ruth Block, she laughed.

Some people didn't trust Eaton's to clear things up for them, so they held on to their items as hostages. This puzzled me, because the store had such a fine reputation. Mary understood the hostage taking as she was a suspicious type herself. She thought I was naïve. So she was kinder to the customers than I was, and more patient, although she still liked to make fun of them.

"I guess old Ruthie's sausage arms have slipped their casings a tad since last time she ordered a blouse," Mary said. "Let's get out of here," she added, glancing up at the clock on the wall. "It's time for lunch."

"It took Ruthie's letter nine days to get to me," I said. "By the time the whole mess is straightened out, summer will be over and she'll have to wait till next spring to wear her new blouse."

"Not your problem, sweetie," said Mary.

"Or maybe we won't even have a size 16."

"Or maybe Ruth's husband will light her on fire and she'll die and blouses won't matter to her anymore," said Mary. "Come on. Let's eat."

We stood up and pushed in our chairs. It was 12:30 on a Friday. We treated ourselves on Fridays to a meal at Moores across the street.

"Enjoy lunch, Rich Girl," a woman named Henny called out from her desk across the room near the windows.

There were some in the office who, like Gwen's mum, resented me for having a job when my family didn't need the money. I didn't know how to argue with them.

"Ignore her," said Mary. "She's a horse's ass," she added loudly. Henny stood up and someone put a hand on her arm.

The heels of our shoes made lovely clopping sounds on the wooden floor as we hurried down the hall toward the stairs. I concentrated on those sounds and tried not to let Henny's words get to me. Maybe she and Gwen's mum were right: I should give my job up to someone who really needed it.

Mary and I stopped on the shipping floor to see if Lester Sykes wanted to join us; often he did. Today he had his hands full with a tiller part.

"It looks to have been damaged after delivery," he said. Someone was trying to get away with something. Poor Lester. He sat at his desk staring at the part; he shook his head and sighed. There were little chunks of dry Manitoba gumbo on his desk.

"Thanks, girls," Lester said. "But I brought my lunch today." He pointed to his battered lunch box. "Maybe next Friday, eh."

Lester was far from a frivolous spender. Mary had told me that he sent as much money as he could possibly manage home to his folks on their farm near Clearwater.

We went for lunch and left Lester to his stewing over his tiller. I had a bacon and tomato sandwich and Mary had sliced turkey. I loved going for lunch at Moores; it made me feel grown-up, like the well-turned-out woman on my imagined train ride with her stream of witticisms. We both dressed with a little more care on Fridays, although neither of us would ever admit it.

It was easier to act sophisticated when Lester wasn't with us leaving a trail of sawdust and dirt behind him. We drank in the appreciative glances of the businessmen, pretending that we didn't notice them and also making believe that we weren't soaked with perspiration beneath our clothes. We both pinned dress shields inside our blouses so the world wouldn't know about our sweat.

Mary was a few years older than me and sometimes wore an engagement ring on her left hand — just sometimes because it turned her finger green. Her boyfriend's name was Perry Toole and I was sure he bought the ring at Woolworth's or worse. She called him her fiancé, which I found embarrassing on her behalf. He didn't look like a fiancé the few times I had seen him. He looked like a hayseed and I was sure Mary could do better.

Perry worked as a hired hand on a farm near their hometown of Carman. Sometimes he drove eggs in to the grading department in the mail-order building. On those days Mary ate lunch with him at the coffee bar in the farmers' waiting room and made sure to wear her ring. She talked about him as though he were king of the world.

"Perry's coming to pick me up at 5:00," she said now. "He's taking me out for supper before we leave the city."

She went home to Carman every weekend.

"What's he driving?" I asked. That was mean, but at least I didn't ask who was paying for supper.

"I don't know," Mary said. "Something, I'm sure." She dabbed her lips matter-of-factly with her cloth napkin.

Last time he came to get her he'd hitched a ride in and Mary'd had to pay for both of them to go home on the train. I wouldn't put up with it if I were her, but she thought she was in love and wouldn't hear a word against him. So I bit my tongue.

He didn't treat her very well as far as I ever saw. He ordered her around and criticized her appearance. Once I heard him tell her that she needed a chocolate milkshake like she needed another hole in her head. Mary had set the milkshake aside. How could she enjoy it after that?

When I asked her what it was about him that she loved so much she said, "He's good to me."

I guess that meant he didn't slam her into walls or light her on fire.

My hope was that Mary would one day break free from Perry. They still hadn't set a date, which I found encouraging.

Even Lester would be a better deal for her. Or maybe one of our lunchtime businessmen would sweep her off her feet. We should stop so studiously ignoring them. I suggested to Mary that she smile at a man with brown wavy hair who made no secret of the fact that he admired her. She did so as we walked out past his table and he smiled back. We laughed all the way back to Eaton's.

The next letter on my pile was from a woman in Roblin, Manitoba. She complained that the colour of her cardigan, or cardy, as she called it, wasn't as described in the catalogue. A vague complaint like that was difficult for me. She had been expecting the light blue of a prairie sky, she wrote, not the light blue of her dead mother's eyes. That letter was beyond me on the first reading. I put it at the bottom of the pile. Maybe later in the day I could come up with an answer for her.

Later in the day I decided that it could wait till Monday.

I walked home after work, over the Main Street Bridge and the Norwood Bridge to our home on Ferndale Avenue. When I got there I found my dad with Mr. Larkin, who lived down the street, staring at a pile of lumber in the backyard.

Dad had been talking lately about building a garage. He didn't like to see his new automobile covered with bird droppings and sap from our neighbours' Manitoba maple, not to mention the ever-present dust that worked its way inside.

"It doesn't smell like a new car anymore," my dad had complained a few days earlier. "It smells like dust."

A worker from Toupin Lumber had delivered the wood and Mr. Larkin offered to help. He was an English professor at the University of Manitoba, so was off on summer holidays.

My dad was taking a few weeks away from the office. Things were slow for him that summer. He worked mostly in property law, sometimes trusts and estates. Few people were buying land in the summer of 1936; few people were buying anything, just trying desperately to hold on to what they had. Dad felt a little guilty about the shiny Buick in our backyard at a time when so many were in dire straits.

"All the more reason to put it inside a garage," I had said when he brought it up.

We had lived through the coldest winter on record that year. That was what got him started on it. He didn't use the car in the bitter cold — he walked to St. Mary's Road where he caught a streetcar — but he convinced himself it needed shelter whether he drove it or not.

So there they stood: the attorney and the professor. My dad couldn't help his lawyerly look, his work clothes being former suit pants that had turned shiny and were frayed at the edges and a scruffy white shirt that Aunt Helen had cut off and hemmed above the elbows. Mr. Larkin wore overalls but they were brand new without a stain on them, and his scholarly glasses, graceful hands, and cheerful poetic quotes gave him away. Neither of them had ever approached a manual labour job of that magnitude.

It was nearly time for supper. Helen was inside, busy with cold roast beef and salad preparations.

"We can't begin now," said my dad. "Let's leave it till tomorrow, shall we, and get a good early start?"

"Right then, Will. That makes sense to me." Hedley Larkin rubbed his perfectly clean hands against the spotless cloth of his overalls.

There was something about beginning in the late afternoon that didn't sit well with either man, even though there were hours of daylight left. My theory was that they had no idea where to begin.

CHAPTER 3

They started work the next morning, a hot cloudless Saturday. At lunchtime on that first day I took salmon sandwiches and iced tea out to them on a tray. They looked to have rearranged some lumber and scratched out a drawing or two in pencil on a scrap of paper, but they hadn't cut a single piece of wood or hammered one nail by that time.

As I drew near, I heard them discussing the ideas of Bertrand Russell. They were talking about machines and emotions and whether they could exist together side by side. Or something like that. Maybe the Buick had set them off; pretty much anything could. Mr. Larkin was consulting a book: *Skeptical Essays* it was called.

"I'm going to leave this with you, Will," he said. "I know you'll enjoy it as much as I did."

"Ah, Violet," said my dad when he saw me coming. "Just the ticket. Ready for a bite, Hedley?"

They sat under the branches of the poplar tree to eat their lunch. The mosquitoes were frightful in the shade but preferable to the relentless dusty rays of the sun. Both men had slathered Potter and Moore's anti-mosquito cream on any exposed skin.

Two figures approached from the lane; they moved slowly in the steamy noonday heat. It became clear to us as we watched them come closer that they were strangers, two men feeling the weight of their journey. When they were near enough to see the pile of wood they offered their help.

"Is it a garage you are to build?" said the older of the two, speaking with a French-Canadian accent.

This type of offer wasn't unusual. There were countless men on the move looking for any kind of work and often they travelled in pairs. These two didn't have the look of tramps. There was a keen light reflecting from the eyes of the one who did the talking. It seemed to shine off their surfaces more than from any depth. Like off flat blue glass. I wanted to understand that but I didn't want to stare. He was perhaps twenty-nine years old and so thin I couldn't get a sense of the shape of him inside his clothes.

"I worked as a builder in Montreal till not so many weeks ago," he said. "Till the work ends. My friend and me, we are going to Alberta. We hear there are sugar beets to hoe."

Men from the east went west; men from the west went east. Little opportunity awaited them in either direction.

When I looked at the friend something shifted inside of me, as if my intestines were sorting themselves out in a new way. He appeared to be eighteen or so with a darkish complexion, light brown hair, and deep chocolate eyes. I loved the lightness of his hair. He wasn't very tall, perhaps about my height — five foot seven. He was sturdy, healthy-looking, didn't look like he had been suffering any from life on the road. Also, his rucksack was well-made and looked quite new, as if he had just bought it for this trip. Maybe he was a pretend rambler, I thought. He was beautiful; I forced myself to look away. He was probably tired of girls staring at him.

"So, you've had some experience then," Mr. Larkin said to the thin man.

"Yes, sir. I have." He moved toward the pile of wood and began to ask questions about dimensions and roof slant.

My dad and Mr. Larkin were stumped by most of his queries but the conversation got them realizing how little they knew about the job ahead of them.

I made it my business to keep the flies off the sandwiches till they were done talking.

"Well, maybe we can work something out," said my dad.

I knew he was struggling. He wanted their help, but he didn't want them staying with us.

"In the meantime," he went on, "have a sandwich. Violet...."
But I was already heading to the house for more of everything.

Aunt Helen came out to meet them. They were eating like
famished refugees.

"Welcome, men," she said. "These two could certainly use the
help." She nodded at my dad and Mr. Larkin.

My dad's face said that he hadn't decided yet, but Aunt Helen
took care of that.

So they stayed. They pitched their tent in the backyard. It was
a bell tent — once white — the kind soldiers used in the Great
War. It was like the tents in Aunt Helen's pictures of those times.
This one was torn in spots and there was evidence of some rough
mending. I saw Helen notice this and knew that she would fix it
for them before they left.

The younger of the two, the handsome one, had no
construction work experience but he assured us that he was a fast
learner and his mate vouched for his good intentions.

"Jesuits teach him," he laughed. "How bad can he be at
anything?"

The handsome one looked as though he would just as soon
not have his Jesuit education out there as public knowledge, but I
think my dad was glad of it. Maybe he thought they could have
some good talks about the sorts of things that concerned Jesuits.
Dad was interested in pretty well everything. As was Mr. Larkin.
That's probably why they were such good friends.

"Did you two meet up on the road?" asked my dad. "Or have
you been friends for longer?"

"No," said the older man. "We met in a camp at Sudbury. We
are both stuck there for some days and we —what are the words?
— hit it off." He smiled.

I knew my dad had way more questions. They were such an
unlikely pair. But he left it at that for now.

He introduced me as his daughter and Helen as his sister so
there wouldn't be any mistaking who was who and what relationship
we all were to each other. It seemed important to him that they
know Helen wasn't his wife. Helen was nine years older than my

dad. He had come along when my grandparents no longer expected him.

The men settled in to our backyard and worked on the garage and ate my aunt's meals and used our bathroom.

After dark that first night I stared for a long time out my bedroom window at the tent. Moths collided with the screen over and over again and left their silken dust behind. I wondered if they would die without it. The murmur of the men's voices and the smell of smoke from their hand-rolled cigarettes wafted up on the muggy moonlit air.

The worst that could happen, I figured, was that they would kill the three of us in our beds and rob us of all our valuables. Or no, they would kill Dad and Helen and leave me deaf, dumb, blind, and paralyzed, but with my brain intact.

They worked all day Sunday. No one among them seemed to have any qualms about working on the Sabbath. I could see it made my dad nervous, but only because of the neighbours.

When Mrs. McTavish walked by on her way to church he waved to her and called, "Good morning, Mrs. McTavish! Pretty hot already, eh?"

She rewarded him with a tightening of her lower facial muscles.

"You get your work done when you can, I guess," he said a little less heartily. He sighed and wiped his brow with a handkerchief as she tottered off on her stout church-going legs.

"Don't worry, Dad," I said. "Mrs. McTavish is an old boot."

She had been my Sunday school teacher when I was younger and she was far too strict for a United Protestant. I think her parents had been something else, Baptists maybe, or Methodists, a type of religion where neither fun nor work was allowed on Sunday. But there weren't all that many churches to choose from in our neighbourhood, just the United, the Anglican, and the Catholic, as far as I knew, and maybe one or two odd duck religions housed in grimy basements.

The other men were oblivious to my dad's discomfort, even Mr. Larkin, who hummed "Comin' Thro the Rye" quietly to himself as he measured and marked the lumber according to Benoit's directions. That was the name of the older man, the one who had been a builder in Montreal: Benoit Bateau, or Benny Boat as I called him to myself.

His friend, the Jesuit, was called Jackson Shirt. I guess either Jesuits worked on Sundays or Jackson was struggling inside without letting on. Or maybe he was a lapsed Jesuit. He didn't look like he was struggling. My best guess was that Jesuits worked on Sundays. I pictured them in long brown robes like Friar Tuck working together in manly camaraderie in a forest without any women looking down their noses at them like the righteous Mrs. McTavish.

Jackson said "ouch" quite often and even "dang" once or twice as he missed a nail with the hammer my dad had provided for him. But he didn't swear out loud and his small outbursts were fewer and farther between as the day wore on.

That night, their second night, I crept downstairs, stole my dad's pack of Sweet Caporals and took them out to the front steps. It was as close to the men as I dared go. They were out back but we breathed in the same dusty lilac air.

A dog barked from way across the night. Maybe it was choking on the dust. Topsoil covered everything; it rode in on the hot wind from the prairies where the farmers' crops would come to nothing. It didn't have to be this way, according to Mr. Larkin. The natural turf of the prairies should have been used only for grazing. When the farmers ploughed it under the way they did there was nothing left to hold the soil in place and the wind blew it away. He said that the misuse of the land in that way was the main cause of the dust storms.

A dark figure startled me as it moved clear of the shadows. It was Jackson, stepping out from beneath the willow tree. I hoped I hadn't been mumbling aloud about Hedley Larkin's agricultural theories.

"Hello," he said.

"Hi. You scared me, looming up like that."

"Can't sleep?" he asked.

"Mmm, no. It's pretty hot upstairs."

"It's pretty hot everywhere," he said.

"Yeah."

His voice was quiet; I had to strain to hear him. I loved his voice.

"I don't sleep," he said.

"Not ever?"

"Not ever."

"I don't believe you," I said.

He smiled and I loved his smile.

"Can I have one of those?" He pointed to the tailor-made cigarettes sitting on the step beside me.

"Sure." I had stolen them for him.

He had a wooden match in his shirt pocket. He got it going with one hand and no aids other than his fingernail. I cringed.

"What's the matter?" he asked.

"I don't like fingernails," I said. "I have a thing about them."

He moved to light my cigarette for me. I cupped my hand around the flame and looked into his eyes as he did it. I'd seen someone do that in a movie. Maybe it was Bette Davis in *Dangerous*. Jackson's eyes were on mine, so the cigarette didn't catch the flame. Real slick, the both of us. He lit another one and this time we got the job done.

"What kind of a thing about fingernails?" he asked.

"It's nothing," I said, wishing I hadn't mentioned it.

He took my hand, the one without the cigarette, and with his thumb tried to push back the fingernail on my index finger. I snatched my hand away and he smiled again.

"I know someone else who doesn't like that," he said.

"Who?"

"No one. A faraway friend."

I noticed that his smoking fingers were stained an ochre colour, like my friend Isabelle's. My best friend, Gwen, didn't smoke, and she thought I was an idiot for trying it.

Mr. Steeples from three doors down walked slowly by with his cane and his cigar. I know he saw us but he didn't say hello. I could feel his displeasure. What was it for? I wondered. What was so great about him and so bad about us? I wanted to shout out that Jackson was a Jesuit.

"How old are you?" I asked Jackson, after the pale darkness had swallowed up Mr. Steeples.

"The same as you."

"How old am I?" I asked.

"You don't know how old you are?"

"Yes, but I don't believe that you know."

"You don't believe a lot," he said.

"I do if people tell me the truth," I said.

"Seventeen."

He sat down on the grass too far away. I wanted him closer; I wanted to breathe his dark skin.

"Me or you?" I said.

"Both of us."

"How do you know that?"

"I'm right, aren't I?"

"Maybe not."

He was right. He laughed. I couldn't see his face in the shadows.

"What's it like being a Jesuit?" I asked.

"I'm not a Jesuit," he said. "I just went to a Jesuit school — a school run by Jesuits."

"Oh." I didn't want him to be ordinary. Please don't be ordinary.

"Kind of like if you were to go to a school run by nuns," he said.

"Oh. Like St. Mary's Academy," I said.

"Whatever."

"Did you wear a uniform?" I asked.

"Yeah."

"What was it like?" I asked. "I can't picture you in a tie."

He chuckled and at the same time I heard the screen door open behind me.

"Violet?" It was my dad.

"Yes."

"What are you doing out there?"

I could hear the contained panic in his voice.

"Nothing. Talking," I said.

"You better come in."

"Talking about Jesuit school," I went on, almost certain that wouldn't make it okay.

It didn't.

Jackson was silent. I wished he would speak, say something innocent and upright.

"Yes, all right," I said when the quietness became too much. I stood up and smoothed my skirt.

None of us said goodnight. It would have seemed phony, out of place.

My dad locked both doors behind us, something he seldom did.

"Keep your distance, Violet. We don't know these men very well."

"Jackson isn't a man. He's seventeen."

"He's a man, all right. Now, go on upstairs."

I couldn't sleep. I looked out my bedroom window at the tent. Someone was humming quietly. Jackson. It was something with a pretty melody, a song from the radio. I wanted to know him. I wanted to know him through and through. He seemed like the world to me, the whole wide world that I didn't know at all.

Chapter 4

In the morning the Sweet Caps were still on the steps. I was glad; I very badly didn't want Jackson to be a thief.

The men weren't up when it was time for me to leave for work. Aunt Helen had made breakfast so she prepared a tray for them and handed it to me.

"Run this out to them, would you, Violet? Maybe it'll help them get a move on." She fussed with the tea towel that covered the biscuits. "It's high time they were up and around."

My dad seized the tray from my hands without a word and took it out to the backyard. I followed him and set off down the lane.

"Breakfast is ready, men," he announced in an unfamiliar voice.

"Thanks, Mr. Palmer." It was Jackson who replied. He sounded wide awake. Maybe he was waiting around for Benny to wake up, not wanting to show him up.

I did a little hop, skip, and jump as I made my way to St. Mary's Road to catch a streetcar downtown.

Mary fussed all day long about her weekend with Perry.

"He doesn't want kids," she said. "I had no inkling of this before Friday night."

"Hmm," I said.

"I want kids more than I want Perry." She rubbed the green stain on her ring finger.

It was important for me not to show my pleasure. "I'm so sorry, Mary," I said. "But I know someone spectacular will come along who'll want the same things that you do."

"All I've ever wanted is kids."

"They can cause a lot of heartache, you know," I said. I had told Mary about Sunny and all that had happened.

"I won't lose my babies," she said and then felt bad for the rest of the day. She couldn't apologize enough and I let her keep trying till the five o'clock scramble for the door.

When I got home from work I sat in the shade of the poplar and watched them build. For most of the day our next door neighbours' maple tree shaded the area where they worked.

Benny Boat really seemed to know what he was doing and he ordered the others around. But he never stopped calling my father "sir," which was good. No one wanted my dad to feel as though he had lost control of anything.

Jackson Shirt didn't have to work very hard to win my heart. He almost had it the first time I saw him. Sometimes after hammering a nail in successfully, he glanced over at me and smiled. I smiled back. When my dad caught this he tried to find something else for me to do.

"Violet, why don't you go inside and see if Helen needs a hand with supper?"

We ate with the men that evening at the picnic table in the backyard. It was cooler there in the shade of the trees than it was in the house. Mr. Larkin couldn't stay.

"Are you sure, Hedley?" Helen said. "We'd love to have you."

"And I'd love to stay." He smiled. "But Enid would skin me alive if she roasted a chicken and I wasn't there to eat it."

The Larkins had no children, so it was up to him alone to enjoy her meals.

My dad cleaned himself up for supper. Both the visiting men washed their hands and faces, but they were getting pretty stinky by this time.

It occurred to me that they must be wondering where my dad's wife was, my mother. But I didn't know how to fit it into the conversation so I thought I'd leave it to my dad or Helen. I didn't think it was any of their business where Sunny was. They had no reason to suspect that she existed, but they must have been curious about my mother.

"My mother is dead," I blurted out. So much for leaving it to one of the others. "She died almost eleven years ago."

"Violet," said my dad and covered my hand with his.

"Well, I thought they might be wondering where she was. I didn't want them thinking she ran away on us or anything." They didn't have to know how she died.

Jackson flushed a deep red all the way down into his open-necked shirt.

And Benoit said, "Sorry. So sorry. I am...you miss her."

Jackson nodded as though to say, "Me too." And gradually his colour returned to normal.

I thought he must have found my bluntness about my mother's death embarrassing. A lot of people I knew found talk of death to be difficult.

We piled our plates high with bubble and squeak.

I loved it; it was one of my favourite suppers, but I was afraid that one or both of our men wouldn't like cabbage. It seemed to me a risky food to serve to guests. I'd heard of people who hated cabbage; for instance, Mary's horrible Perry hated it. It reminded him of bohunks, he'd said. Watching the way both men shovelled it in, I saw I had nothing to worry about.

Besides, as Helen had said to me in the kitchen when I voiced my concerns, "They're not guests; they're hired hands. They'll eat what's put in front of them."

"If you fellows would like to have baths, please go ahead," she said now to shift the talk away from my mother's death.

To use the bathroom they needed to go upstairs to the second storey of the house where our bedrooms were. That seemed almost unbearably familiar to me and I wondered how my dad could stand it.

"You should find everything you need in the bathroom," she went on.

"Thank you, ma'am," the men said in unison and then laughed.

My dad squirmed, but thank goodness he held his tongue.

"We both need a good wash," Benoit said, a little discomfited, I guess, knowing we were conscious of the pungent odour fixed to them both like a second skin.

Later that evening I was in my bedroom reading an old issue of *McCall's*. It contained an article about unladylike behaviour that had caught my eye.

Jackson was the first to have a bath. I heard him running a tub and scrupulously cleaning it afterwards. I loved that he did that. If he hadn't, I would have, just to see what sort of dirt he left behind.

"The Dutch Cleanser is almost empty, ma'am." I heard him say this to Aunt Helen when he went downstairs.

"Thank you, dear," she said. "I'll pick some up tomorrow. I have some other shopping to do."

We had a Dutch Cleanser backup. I knew we did. Aunt Helen wasn't the type of housekeeper who ran out of things that were possible to get. She was just being kind, making Jackson feel as though he was being helpful. I wanted to ruin it by shouting out, "We've got a backup, you morons!" But I didn't, of course.

I wished I could call him "dear" like Aunt Helen did. It was easy for her: she was in her forties.

"Is there anything either of you boys would like?" she asked. "My meals aren't very fancy, I know."

So much for her "they'll eat what I put in front of them" statement, I thought. And when did her "men" turn into "boys"?

"Your meals are plenty fancy for us, ma'am," Jackson said. "You're a wonderful cook. Good healthy meals."

I heard Helen giggle and I imagined an accompanying blush. A sick slop water feeling flipped my insides and took me by surprise. I hustled down the stairs to insinuate my skinny presence into the kitchen where they were talking.

Jackson's long hair was wet and combed straight back from his face. Always after his baths — he quickly got into the habit of taking one every evening — his hair started out that way and then softened and curled around his handsome face.

Benoit wasn't so keen on baths. He thought Jackson overdid it. My dad thought so too.

CHAPTER 5

We settled into a kind of routine. The men worked all day on the garage. Mr. Larkin came by most days and helped a little, but more often than not he and Dad would sit under the poplar, drinking orange Kik and chatting about Mackenzie King or the old age pension or the "Fred Allen Show" that they had both listened to on the radio on Sunday night. And Benoit and Jackson sawed and hammered away.

I went to work and hurried home so that I could help Helen with supper and hang around the men as much as I could without upsetting my dad. Everybody ate well and there was a certain peace around the place with small pockets of restlessness and worry rearing up from time to time: the restlessness from me and the worry from my dad.

"What's a boy like Jackson doing on the road?" he asked Helen one evening. They were sitting on the verandah and didn't know I was listening through an open window.

"Why don't you ask him?" Helen said.

"He has as much as admitted that he comes from a family that's well-to-do," my dad went on. "They live in the Westmount area of Montreal, for heaven's sake. Why would he want to throw his lot in with all the desperate men on the road looking for work when he doesn't have to?"

"Maybe he just wants to get a taste of the country at large, gain experience," Helen said, "see how the other half lives."

"But we aren't really the other half, are we? We're probably not all that different from his own family, class-wise, I mean."

"Well, his exploits aren't likely to end with us, are they, Will? The boys talk about heading out to hoe sugar beets after the garage is finished. That's darned hard work. Do you think that would be a difficult enough job to suit your needs for Jackson?"

"Don't be ridiculous, Helen."

"You're the one being ridiculous, Will. If you want explanations from the boy, for goodness' sake, ask him. I seriously doubt there's anything sinister about his motivations. But I certainly don't have any answers for you."

"Why would anyone choose to ride the rails if he didn't have to?" Will went on. "I just don't get it."   .

"Maybe there's nothing to get," said Helen.

He let it go for the time being, didn't mention it again for a while, but I'm sure it was stewing around inside his head.

Helen and the two visiting men-boys and Mr. Larkin moved about in the heavy air like the inhabitants of a watercolour. They felt the heat, certainly, but seemed easy with it and appeared oblivious to the idea that anything could threaten this time of safety and wellness and work. It wasn't an especially pretty watercolour, but endlessly interesting, to me, anyway. I'd for sure have hung it on a wall.

My aunt was glad of the extra company around the place. She grumbled good-naturedly to my dad about the added work, but she didn't mean it. She was blooming. My dad and I weren't enough for her after her nursing adventures. Before the Queen Charlottes she had been back at the Royal Victoria Hospital in Montreal for a year upgrading her skills. That's where she had taken her training. It gave her something else to talk to "the boys" about. I even heard her fumbling about in French with Benny one time.

Both men were bilingual. French was Benny's first language and he struggled some with English. English was Jackson's first language but I didn't know if he spoke French with an English accent. It didn't sound to me like he did. I asked Benny and he didn't seem to know what I was talking about.

I couldn't decide in those first days if Benny was dim-witted or really smart. He seemed to vacillate between the two. I came to realize that the apparent dullness was more like a trance that he slipped into where he wouldn't or couldn't acknowledge the world around him.

At night I would hear the two of them murmuring together from inside the tent, sometimes into the wee hours. I couldn't help but wonder what they found to talk about for so long and so seriously.

Benny knew an awful lot about many things, like building, for one, and geography, for another. When he wasn't in a trance he could be very talkative. On more than one occasion I heard him and Aunt Helen talking about the ocean life off the Queen Charlotte Islands.

And he went off on tangents that sometimes sucked me right in. He told me that he believed that all of time — past, present, and future — existed at once, together. The linear passage of time was an illusion, he said. And if you believed with all your might and trained hard you could move through holes in the atmosphere into the future and into the past. It was a matter of concentration, he said, and being able to identify and connect with a portal, an entryway.

In other words, he believed in time travel. He hadn't managed it yet, but he spent a lot of time sitting quietly on his own and he explained to me that during those times he was preparing himself for a trip, a sideways trip. He was convinced and he almost convinced me that it would happen someday. So that was what his trances were all about.

The past interested him more than the future, as it did me. I wanted to travel through time too. Who wouldn't? But I couldn't quite believe in it so I didn't bother trying to train. I figured I'd wait and see if Benny met with any success before I went that far.

He nagged me some about it because I didn't have the heart to tell him that I was pretty sure his idea was daft. He wanted me to sit with him but I always came up with excuses not to: my dad wants me to wash the car, Aunt Helen asked me to bake cookies,

Gwen invited me over to see their new pups. It was always someone else's fault that I couldn't take the time to go into trances with him. That way he couldn't talk me out of my excuses.

Gwen lived one street over on Lawndale Avenue. Her brother's dog, Tippy, had indeed had pups, but that was over a year ago now and they had all been given away.

There weren't all that many houses at Gwen's end of Lawndale in 1936; it was just a dirt road that edged onto the field next to the golf course. When we were younger we'd hunted for golf balls on summer days. Then we would try and sell them back to the golfers who were generally pretty good about humouring us with some coins. It seemed like it was mostly rich people who golfed, so we didn't feel bad about taking their money. I still felt like scouting for balls sometimes; it was fun. But we were too old now for that type of play. It was best left to the younger kids like Gwen's brother Warren and his friends.

I could always use Gwen as an excuse to get away from Benny and his ideas. She was fully in the picture. I hadn't told her how I felt about Jackson, though. Those feelings were too fragile to voice. It would take almost nothing to wound them. Also, he had asked me what her name was once after she had been at our house; he had noticed her. Gwen was a lot prettier than I was and I decided it was best if I kept them apart.

I wondered what Jackson's thoughts were on time travel. He wouldn't give me an answer when I asked.

He just said, "Benoit is really smart. I'm lucky to have hooked up with him." Once he even said, "I think it was meant to be that Benoit and I found each other in Sudbury."

That sounded religious to me; whether Jesuit-related or not, I didn't know.

My best guess was that Jackson was skeptical about the time travel business, but he admired Benny and didn't want to admit to doubting him so he went along with him on his tangents. Quietly. He had found a good travelling companion, which couldn't have been easy, and he didn't want to jeopardize that in any way.

Also, he didn't want to commit either to strange beliefs or to any kind of narrow-mindedness. He was, after all, only seventeen. My age. How much more than me could he possibly know? Lots, maybe. He'd had way more experience than I'd had, that's for sure. But I felt as though I was as smart as Jackson, just not as self-assured. It was self-assurance that gave people the appearance of being clever.

During those hot and dusty days one of my jobs when I was around was to make sure the men always had cool clean water to drink and to dip their faces into. My job at Eaton's was really starting to interfere. I wanted to quit, but by now my dad thought it was a good thing: it got me out of Jackson's sight for the working day. He didn't admit to that as a reason. He said he thought the job was good for my self-esteem. I had given him my speech about self-assurance and now he was using it against me.

So it was only on certain days that I could help Aunt Helen with the midday meals. Halfway through the mornings we fed them bread and cheese and fruit.

Jackson called me "miss" in front of my dad.

"Ah. Here's our Violet," Dad would say when the screen door closed after me. Helen held it open till I was safely clear with the tray.

"Thanks, miss." Jackson would wave from his precarious perch on the quickly forming roof of the garage. I wanted to sit with them while they ate, but I saw that my dad was uneasy with that so I left them to it.

CHAPTER 6

On the second Saturday of the men's stay I went over to visit Gwen. The sun beat down on my bare head; I should have worn a hat. The morning was hot and steamy and there was no breeze on the baked streets.

I hoped to find her home alone. I didn't feel much like running into Mrs. Walker. Gwen's mother, Gert, was my least favourite person in the world. Tippy didn't like her either. The dog cowered when she came around and that was proof enough for me that she was genuinely bad.

The air in the yard was heavy, but free of Godawful Gert, as I thought of her. Warren and Tippy were poking around in the backyard.

"Hi, Warren. Hi, Tip."

"Hi, Violet."

I bent down toward Tippy and she leapt up and gave my face a quick lick before settling back down to watch Warren, who had a few old pieces of lumber in front of him, seven dead gophers, an axe, a hammer, and some nails.

"Whatcha doin'?" I asked.

"I'm lookin' for a suitable piece of wood."

"What for?"

"Gopher tails."

Warren was small for his age. I kept thinking he was younger than he was.

He chose the sturdiest piece of wood and tossed the others in the direction of the shed. Then he picked up the axe and chopped the tails off the gophers, one by one. These he began to nail to the wood, in an evenly spaced row.

"Is this some sort of project for Boy Scouts or something?" I asked.

Warren chuckled. "Nah. Scouts is for blockheads." He paused in his hammering. "The manager over at the golf course gives me two cents a tail. The gophers are really chewin' up the course this summer."

"That's really impressive, Warren." I wasn't kidding. "How do you catch them?"

"I pour water down one hole and they come out another. When they do, Tippy grabs 'em in her teeth and breaks their backs. Simple."

"Gosh."

I sat on the stoop and watched him for a while.

"How are the men getting on, building your garage?" he asked.

"Good," I said. "You should come over and watch them sometime."

"I do," he said. "They even let me do the odd thing."

"Really? That's great, Warren! What kinds of things do they let you do?"

"Oh, fetch tools, lug lumber around, stuff like that."

"Golly, that's more than they let me do. All I get to do is bring them food and drink."

"Your dad said mostly you're at work at Eaton's."

"Yeah, rotten old work. I think I'd rather build a garage."

"Building a garage is men's work," said Warren.

"Maybe so," I sighed. "Maybe so." I pictured two of the men, my dad and Mr. Larkin, with their clean fingernails and sunburnt noses. And I pondered divisions of labour, allotment of tasks. There had to be more to it than gender, didn't there?

"Is your mum at home?" I asked Warren quietly.

"Nah. I wouldn't be doin' this here if she was. She'd be yellin' at me that I was lowerin' the tone of the place, makin' us look like Polacks." He shook his head as though that were the craziest notion he'd ever heard.

"What the heck's a Polack?" I asked. I knew but I wanted to hear what Warren would say.

"I dunno. Somethin' that lowers the tone."

When he was done he set off over the field to the golf club with the mounted gopher tails over his shoulder. Tippy went too, veering off to nose about in the scrub.

"What about these dead fellas?" I called out after Warren, looking at the mess he'd left behind. The sight caused a slight queasiness in my stomach.

"I'll bury 'em when I get back," he shouted over his shoulder.

Warren stumbled but caught himself, probably tripping on a gopher hole. Tippy seemed to notice too, and raced back to Warren. She trotted along the rest of the way by his side.

The wind was up again by now. It only ever seemed to die down for short spells or when everyone was in bed and too sleepy to enjoy the calm.

Gwen shouted out the kitchen window for me to come in.

"That's some little brother you have," I said as I sat down at the kitchen table.

She placed a cup of instant coffee in front of me. Maxwell House. "Yeah. He'd be rich if he didn't give all his money to my mum."

I tried to talk about Jackson.

"Hmm," Gwen said, and muttered something else under her breath.

"What?" I said.

She didn't answer and I said it again, louder. "What?"

"Well, don't you think it's kind of...strange having tramps living in your backyard?"

My mouth opened and I stared at her.

"They're not tramps!" I shouted. "Holy Hell, Gwen! You sound like your mother." I felt my face heat up and I began to sweat in a way that wasn't weather-related. "I guess you think they're lowering the tone of the neighbourhood, like Warren's gophers."

"Don't yell," Gwen said.

I got up and paced the small kitchen floor. I felt sick.

"Your face is all blotchy," said Gwen.

Jackson didn't fit into the world that she and I occupied together. I wondered for a second if it would make a difference to her that he came from a wealthy family in Westmount. But I wasn't going to try to explain him or excuse him. It was Gwen and her mother that were the low-life scum.

"I hope to God your mum doesn't succeed in poisoning Warren like she has you," I said. "He said 'Polack' a few minutes ago."

"So?"

This was the worst fight Gwen and I had ever had. In fact, I didn't think we'd had one before. When I realized that I was the only one doing the fighting I sat back down.

"Your mum isn't home, is she?" I whispered to Gwen, double-checking.

"No. We wouldn't be having coffee if she was. But you don't have to be scared of her. She doesn't hate you or anything."

"I wish you wouldn't listen to her mean ways," I said, stirring my coffee. "She's unchristian-like."

Gwen laughed. "Since when do you know so much about unchristian-like behaviour?"

"Since forever," I said. "That's what Sunday school was for. Maybe you should have gone more often."

I sipped my coffee. "This tastes like poo," I said. All that cream and sugar and it still wasn't any good. Gwen made terrible coffee — weak — I guess so Gert wouldn't notice that any was gone.

"It's not that I'm scared of her," I went on, realizing for the first time that I was. "I just think she thinks I'm a bad influence on you and that's so boneheaded. She's the one that's a bad influence."

Gwen ignored that. "Fraser Foote wants to go out with you," she said.

"How do you know?" I took one last sip and pushed my coffee aside.

"He told Dirk."

"Well, why doesn't he tell me?"

"He wanted Dirk to get me to feel you out on the subject. Apparently he doesn't want to ask you out if you're going to say no."

"I like Fraser," I said.

"So you will?"

"I guess so."

"For sure?"

"Yeah, I guess. Why's he such a scaredy cat? That's not very appealing."

"I don't know. Maybe it's because Wilma hurt him so badly when she left him for Quintano."

"How could she like Quint better than Fraser?" I said. "He's so...swarthy."

"Beats me," Gwen said. "I guess she sees something in him. He is a bit of a go-getter."

"Kind of like your brother, but older and with more goop in his hair."

Warren walked in the back door.

"Who's like me?" he asked.

"You don't wear any goop, do you, Squirt?" Gwen said and tousled his dusty hair.

He slipped away from her and made a big production out of counting his earnings at the table. Two nickels and four pennies.

"Fourteen cents," he announced.

Gwen tried to swipe it off the table and he swatted her hand away.

"How old are you now, Warren?" I asked. "Around nine or so?"

"Hell, no," he said. "I'm wearin' on to eleven."

"Yeah, wearin' on to eleven next May," said Gwen. "You're ten years old, Warren. Now go outside and bury those gophers before Mum gets home. She'll throw a fit if she sees them practically lying on top of the horseradish. And don't swear," she called after him.

"Hell isn't a swear word," he yelled back.

"Yes, it is."

"No, it isn't. It's a place."

"Who said?"

"Jackson said."

"See?" Gwen said to me.

"See what?"

"He's been hanging around at your place," Gwen said. "If my mum finds out she'll kill him."

Gwen and Warren didn't have a dad. Mr. Walker had died a long time ago, before Warren was born and before I got to know the family. That's all I knew: their dad was dead. No details. Gwen wouldn't let me bring up the topic of dead fathers, especially around her mother. I suspected that it wasn't true that her dad had died. I don't think she ever had one. My theory was that Gert Walker was a slattern in her younger days and had two kids by different fathers. Maybe she had even been a prostitute. That's probably how she had saved enough money to buy the tiny house on Lawndale Avenue.

Now she was a cleaner at Earl Grey School. And she thought she knew everything. I shuddered to think. She probably taught the kids who passed her in the halls to be mean to those less fortunate than themselves and, why not? to those more fortunate as well.

During the summer months she cleaned houses to make extra money. That's probably where she was now, at a big lemon-scented house in Crescentwood, polishing newel posts and scrubbing toilets. I didn't usually mention it because it embarrassed Gwen that her mum cleaned other people's houses.

But now I said, "So is Gert on scrubwoman duty today?"

Gwen pretended she didn't hear me. She was next to impossible to get a rise out of.

It would have been great if Gwen had had a mother that I liked. I had Aunt Helen, but it seemed to me that you could never have too much in the good-mother department.

I stood up to leave.

"Okay," Gwen said. "So the official word is that you will say yes if Fraser asks you out."

"Well, I don't know about official. What if I'm doing something else when he wants to go out, what if I'm time travelling, what if I die, what if the world ends, what if he dies?"

"I'm going to tell Dirk that you'll say yes."

"Dirk's a gink," muttered Warren as he let the screen door slam behind him.

"Wash your hands," said Gwen.

I laughed, but didn't say that I agreed with Warren. Gwen thought for some reason that the sun shone out of Dirk's rear end, probably just because he was good-looking to her way of thinking and his dad was a city official of some kind who cut the occasional ribbon.

Dirk wasn't ugly, but his even features often had a sour look to them, the type of expression where if he lived at our house my dad would say, "If you're not careful your face will stay that way."

And his hair was too short, his lips were too thin, and his trousers were pulled up way too high. Also, his voice had no rise and fall to it; he sounded like a corpse would sound if it could talk. He disturbed me.

"Tippy doesn't like him," Warren said. "She growls when he comes around."

"Be quiet," said Gwen.

"Does she like Fraser Foote?" I asked Warren.

"I don't know if she's met him," said Warren, "but I like Fraser. He's a good egg. He helped me fix my wagon once when a wheel fell off near his house."

"Yeah, he is a good egg," I said. "I'll see you folks later."

As I walked home it occurred to me that I didn't like either Mary's boyfriend or Gwen's. Was I just jealous because they were attached, because they had someone to hold their hands in public? People said "Mary and Perry" or "Gwen and Dirk" in the same breath. They were couples. It seemed unlikely that I would ever be part of a couple, a taken-for-granted part of a couple. But I also knew that, as Warren said, Dirk Botham was a gink, if not worse, and Perry Toole was a gink for sure.

"Violet and Jackson," I said out loud. I liked the sound of it. "Violet and Fraser," I tried next. That sounded good too, but it didn't light up the inside of me in quite the same way.

My friend Isabelle wasn't part of a couple. She had no time for that, what with helping to support her family and looking after her brother and sisters. During the school year she collected cardboard boxes in her spare time. There wasn't big money in it, but maybe a bit more than in gopher tails. Boys liked Is; she was an adventuress. But I think they were afraid of her, too; at least the boys I knew.

She lived in a rough-and-tumble apartment block on Taché Avenue. Her family was way poorer than even the Walkers. Gert would look down on her for sure.

My step lightened as I thought of a possible date with Fraser. Then I grew achy with thoughts of Jackson. My body had no doubt where I wanted to be, however hard my brain fought it.

"Hey there, Skipper," shouted Jackson from high on the ladder.

"Hi, young fella," called Benoit from the door he was framing.

I turned around and realized that Warren had followed me home.

CHAPTER 7

By the end of the weekend, the garage was nearing completion. At lunchtime on the hot and windy Sunday Helen held the door for me as usual and then went back inside. I carried a tray piled high with ham and lettuce sandwiches.

The eyes of all the men turned towards me. Jackson was at the very top of the wooden ladder. He turned too quickly and too far and he fell, slowly, it seemed to me, with his arms stretched out in front of him.

"No, don't!" It was his arms that caused me to shout. He was going to land all wrong.

He hit the hard dirt and we all heard the crack of bone breaking. I put the tray down on the stoop. We all rushed to his crumpled form.

"Helen!" shouted my dad.

Jackson had landed hands first. His eyes were closed and I thought for a moment he was dead. I crouched down beside him. Aunt Helen flung herself out the back door and over to where we had all gathered.

"Oh, my land!" she said and knelt down next to me. "He's broken both his arms." She smoothed the hair back from his forehead where dirt mixed with sweat. I wished I had done that, but I was paralyzed with fear and love and not wanting to upset my dad.

"All right, Jackie dear," said Aunt Helen.

Jackie. I didn't like that.

She took off her apron and then mine and tenderly secured his arms to his body so they wouldn't flop around.

"Let's you men get him into the Buick," she said, "and we'll take him to the hospital."

"Rotten Buick," I said and my dad looked at me, bewildered.

If it weren't for the car none of this would have happened. But if it weren't for the car and the garage Jackson wouldn't be here and I never would have met him at all. Yes, I would have. We were meant to be, as he said he and Benoit were. I believed that.

As the garage had taken shape I had been dreading Jackson's departure. I had even devised a scheme where I would scout the neighbourhood for Benny and him, drumming up business. I had already approached Mr. Foote, Fraser's dad, about his dilapidated shed. That was before I knew Fraser wanted to ask me out. Mr. Foote was still thinking about it. I was sure if I kept at him he would come around.

But Jackson would be out of commission for at least six weeks. I knew how broken arms worked; I'd had one of my own when I was twelve.

"For God's sake, be careful with him," Helen said with her hands covering the lower part of her face as the men clumsily placed him on the back seat of the car. That was the first time I ever heard her use the name God in that way.

It was decided that she would go with my dad and Jackson to St. Boniface Hospital.

"I'm a nurse," she said.

"Big deal," I said quietly.

Helen set herself up in the back seat with Jackson's head resting on her shoulder. At her orders I ran inside for a cold cloth and she held it against his forehead as they drove off.

Benny and Mr. Larkin and I sat with the lunch tray, but we didn't eat. We sipped lemonade for a while and then the men went quietly back to work. I put a tea towel over the sandwiches and took them inside to the fridge. I'd offer them again later after the horror had died down.

I was positive that all of us were thinking about the same thing: how was Jackson, with casts on both arms, going to feed himself, wash himself, dress himself, hold himself to pee, wipe his bum after using the toilet? Dad and Aunt Helen would be thinking it, too, as they bumped down Taché Avenue to the hospital. Jackson may have been lucky enough to lose consciousness for a little while, to save himself from those dreadful thoughts for a short time longer.

But those musings paled next to what I decided was the worst that could happen: Jackson would contract polio while in the hospital, the worst kind, where you can't talk or swallow or breathe, and death is a certainty.

I didn't know anyone personally who had polio but I'd heard about the victims, like I'd heard about the people who died from the heat that summer. Heat prostration was what they called it in the paper when they reported new cases. They even counted the horses, dogs, and cats that died.

It seemed to me that the people who died from the heat always came from the poor side of town. They were the ones who were on relief and lived on streets with names like Alfred and Logan and Battery and Martha. That didn't need any explaining.

But the polio victims usually seemed to come from Ashland and Rosewarne and Chestnut Street, where regular folks like us lived. And that puzzled me. When I mentioned it to Aunt Helen she suggested that perhaps Winnipeg's middle classes were a bit too concerned with cleanliness and didn't give themselves a chance to build up any resistance to the disease.

"What do you mean?" I asked.

"An early exposure to the virus could build up an immunity to it," she said, in her nurse-like fashion, "a protection that people like us might not have because we clean away any chance of that exposure."

I liked that theory. I liked the idea of letting a little dirt build up here and there and having an argument for it.

"Is this true, Helen, or is this something you made up?" I asked at the time.

"It's true and I made it up," she said.

When I had first heard the word *polio*, the same spring that I got stuck in the mud in my new rubber boots, I thought it had a jolly sound to it. Poli-oli-oli-o! Poli-oli-I-over! Like it belonged in one of our skipping songs. But that didn't last long.

The school nurse, Miss Peeler, came into our grade four classroom to tell us how not to get that dreaded disease. It was very contagious, she said. Don't go swimming, stay squeaky clean, and don't hang around with people who aren't. At that point practically everyone in the class turned around to look at Margie Willis because she was the dirtiest person most of us knew. She was the younger sister of the Willis twins, the neighbourhood bad boys. In those days they lived in the same rickety old house on Cromwell Street that they lived in now with their exhausted-looking mother and maybe a grandfather. An old man, anyway. None of us had ever seen a dad, unless the old man was the dad.

Once, when I was walking home from the Piggly Wiggly store, way back when, I passed their house and the grandfather was sitting on the back stoop cutting his toenails. There was nothing unusual about that, I thought, just bad manners doing it outside where anyone could see. What was unusual was the tool he was using to do the job. It was a pair of pruning shears like the ones Dad used to trim the shrubs. Aunt Helen called them secateurs. It made me feel kind of sick. I don't ever want to have toenails so big and coarse that a garden tool is needed to cut them.

Anyway, that day in grade four I forced myself not to turn around and look at Margie Willis. Look at me, how great I am. I'm not staring at the dirty girl.

Some kids made up a song at recess:

Polio Joe, from Mexico
Hands up, stick 'em up, Polio Joe.

That was the extent of it. It was just a redo of some other stupid song about cowboys. I couldn't join in singing it. I knew if I did, I would get polio for sure and end up in braces or worse, like the children in the pictures that Nurse Peeler showed us. The worst that could happen, the worst that polio could do to you, was cause you to not be able to breathe or swallow. In that case, you died.

CHAPTER 8

The hospital kept Jackson for a few nights. There was a reluctance to discharge him until some certainty of his living situation was established. Plaster casts on both arms went up past his elbows. The break in his right arm was near his wrist and less severe than the break in his left. The doctor felt certain that in four weeks the one cast could be replaced by another that would stop below Jackson's elbow, allowing some use of his right arm.

But for the next month he would need help. Aunt Helen insisted that he stay with us. Not in a tent in the backyard, but in the spare bedroom upstairs.

"I am a nurse," she said. "I am more than qualified to look after Jackson's needs."

The "I am a nurse" statement was starting to grate on my nerves but I was rooting for her. Jackson living in our house for at least four weeks!

When Helen made her announcement on the Wednesday following the accident we were eating supper at the dining room table. Potato salad, cold chicken, and peas.

My dad's usually hearty appetite was suffering. He pushed the food around on his plate like he used to get after me not to do. One pea tumbled over the edge and landed on the tablecloth. He pierced it with his fork and placed it back among the others. It left a tiny green stain on the white linen.

"I don't know, Helen," he said. "I don't like the idea of a stranger sleeping down the hall." He glanced at me and pushed a little chunk of potato off his plate.

"For goodness' sake, Will, stop fiddling with your food!" said Helen.

They could have been children again, the small boy and the older sister who was left too soon to look after her little brother. My dad had been only twelve when my grandpa drowned. My grandmother had survived the sinking of the *Titanic* only to die a few months later from pneumonia. So at the age of twenty-one Helen had had to adjust her dreams and plans to accommodate the needs of a twelve-year-old boy.

"Jackson isn't a stranger," she said now. "And it was your rickety old ladder he fell from, Will, your garage he was helping to build."

"He should go home to Montreal," said my dad. "He should be in touch with his parents about this."

"Maybe there's a rift between them," said Helen. "Maybe they're estranged."

"He's too young to be estranged from his parents," Dad said.

"You know better than that, Will."

They both looked at me then as if there was some deep dark secret about familial estrangement that I wasn't supposed to know about.

This fight didn't need me. I gnawed away on my drumstick.

"I'm going to broach it with him," said my dad. "The idea of him speaking to his folks, going home. I could front him a little money if need be."

They were quiet for a while as we dealt in our own ways with the food on our plates.

"What about Benoit?" Dad said quietly.

"Benoit can stay in the tent until the garage is finished and then go or stay as he pleases. He isn't our worry. Jackson is."

My dad didn't like the set-up Helen had in mind; he didn't like it one bit. But he looked up to his older sister and I think he knew deep in his heart that it was the right thing to do. First, though, he insisted on discussing with Jackson the possibility of his heading back east to his family.

Outside the dining room window I could see Benny sitting at the picnic table with his supper in front of him. His eating alone out there seemed wrong somehow, but I knew now wasn't the time to mention it. One stranger at a time.

In the days after Jackson's accident Benny stayed very silent except for his hammering. He went into more trances than usual. I guess he was looking harder than ever for a fissure to slip through that would free him, however briefly, from his difficult life.

The three of us went to the hospital after supper: Dad, Aunt Helen, and me.

We let my dad talk first.

Jackson did not want to go home.

"I can't go back home yet," he said. "I need to complete what I started." He didn't elaborate on what that was and none of us asked. Good manners, I guess. Surely it wasn't work on the garage or hard labour in the sugar beet fields that he cared about finishing.

It seemed to me as though he was trying to prove something to someone, his parents maybe, someone back home who had perhaps accused him of being less than who he was supposed to be. He wanted to show someone what he was made of. A girl? An employer? That was my current theory. Or maybe he didn't want the life that a wealthy background offered him.

He finally coughed up that he lived with his mum in Westmount and that his dad was dead. He had died the previous winter from a massive heart attack. That was as far as he would go. He knew his broken arms changed things drastically, but he said he would rather live with his broken arms in a hobo jungle than go home before he had done what he'd set out to do.

"What exactly is that, Jackson?" asked my aunt. Yay, Helen! I could feel all of our ears perking up.

But Jackson didn't respond. In fact, he closed his eyes and for a moment I thought he had drifted off to sleep.

My dad shook his head slightly from side to side. "We need to contact your mother, Jackson. She at least needs to know what's happened to you." He spoke in a louder than usual voice.

"She's not well," said Jackson.

When he saw the look on my dad's face he quickly added, "She has lots of help."

"I'm afraid I'm going to insist, Jackson. You're only seventeen."

"Yes, all right." He recited the Montreal telephone number. My dad scrambled for a pencil to write it down. He had one in his shirt pocket, along with a tiny leatherbound pad of paper with his initials on it.

"I should mention that my mother wasn't there when I left."

"What do you mean she wasn't there?" asked my dad.

"She sometimes goes to the hospital for extended stays."

No one knew what to say to this, but finally Jackson continued. "She's mentally ill, my mum. She goes to a sanitarium sometimes when she gets really bad."

"I see," said my dad. "Do you have any older brothers or sisters, Jackson?"

"No, sir."

A nurse came in to plump Jackson's pillows and ask him if he needed anything and that gave us all a chance to partially digest this new information. When she left, Aunt Helen began to present her case for Jackson staying on with us in the house.

My dad leapt up from his chair.

"Stop, Helen!" he interrupted. "At least till I've spoken to…someone in Montreal."

He left the room then for a few minutes, maybe to talk to someone at the nurses' station, maybe just to cool down; I don't know.

Helen kept on.

At first Jackson argued against staying with us.

"I couldn't," he said.

"Nonsense!" said Helen. "What else are you going to do if you won't go home? Stay in the hospital? They're likely to insist that you go home."

The reality of what it would be like must have sunk in as the nurses bustled around him taking care of his every need.

"Would you feel more comfortable if I hauled my nurse cap out of storage?" Helen asked.

Jackson smiled. "No, you don't have to do that. But…"

"Don't worry, Jackson," she said. "Don't worry."

"What about Mr. Palmer?" he said.

"You leave him to me," said Helen.

Whatever situation Jackson left behind must be seriously untenable, I thought, for him to entertain the idea of staying with us and allowing Aunt Helen to help him with his private business. And any worries he had about putting us out and withstanding my dad's judgments also seemed to pale in comparison. He was very definite about his mission away from home. Whether it was something he was running from or running to, was impossible to say.

It occurred to me that he might be more comfortable with a man looking after him, like, say, Benoit, but he blanched when I suggested it.

The last thing he said before we left him was, "I'll pay board. I insist on paying room and board."

When we got home my dad called the number Jackson had given him. A woman answered the phone. She introduced herself as Mrs. Dunning, the housekeeper, and said that Mrs. Shirt was not at home. When my dad said he had news about Jackson, the housekeeper kept my dad waiting while she went to confer with someone. The butler? The cook?

Talking on the telephone all the way to Montreal was not cheap. My dad grew more impatient by the second. Finally he started shouting, "Hello!" down the line and Mrs. Dunning finally came back.

"Is Jackson all right?" she asked.

Dad explained about his situation at our house and Jackson's broken arms and he left our number with her. Mrs. Dunning confided that Mrs. Shirt was in a "rest home" indefinitely. She said that she would convey the message to the family lawyer.

"Thank God it's just his arms," she went on.

That struck Helen and me as odd when my dad related what she'd said after he'd hung up in frustration.

"Maybe she's glad it's just his arms because everything else going on in that house is infinitely worse than broken arms," said my dad. "That's what it sounds like to me. Imagine her saying she would pass the message on to the family lawyer!"

"Perhaps the family lawyer is also a family friend," said Helen.

"Perhaps," said my dad.

No one called back.

The next day Helen and I prepared the spare room for Jackson: aired the mattress and the bedspread in the still of early morning during a lull between dusty winds, fitted the bed with clean sheets, chose a few books we thought might interest him. We even put a vase of poppies on the dresser. Helen fetched his knapsack from the tent and rested it at the end of the bed. The knapsack tempted me with its plump contents and secret folds.

That evening, Helen went to the church to help organize tables for a rummage sale. Dad was in the backyard with Benoit. I could hear their hammers and the odd pocket of conversation. I didn't catch much.

Dad: Blah, Mrs. Shirt seems to be blah, blah…

Benoit: He has not blah, blah…about his life blah…We mostly talk about blah, blah….

My dad was obviously trying to pump Benoit for information about the Shirts, but Benoit either had little to give up or he was good at keeping things to himself. I suspected a bit of both.

After I finished doing the dishes I went upstairs and stared at Jackson's knapsack through the open door of his room. There was a tear in the new material that needed sewing up. He wouldn't get very far without losing something, the state it was in. That would be my excuse if I got caught entering the room and emptying the knapsack out on the bedspread: mending intentions.

It was mostly clothes that made up the bulk. The other contents were few. There were two pocket books that looked to have a western flavour — cowboy stories. And a tattered bible. I opened it to the cover page and found this inscription: *To Jackson, from Mummy, 1924.* Maybe she gave it to him the year he headed off to school with the Jesuits. He didn't seem like a bible reader now, but carrying the book with him didn't necessarily mean that he was. He may just have wanted to bring something of his mother with him, odd duck though she seemed to be. It sounded possible from what Jackson had said that she was a full-fledged lunatic.

One page stuck out a little further than the others and when I examined it I found that it wasn't a page at all, but a photograph of a slender young boy that was tucked in for safekeeping. His hair was slicked back from his sad delicate features and he was dressed in his Sunday best. A thin current of recognition zigged through my brain. Was it Jackson in earlier times?

I turned the picture over and found the same writing that inscribed the bible: *"Bertram" (1935)*, it read. It must be Jackson's younger brother, I thought. He hadn't said he didn't have any younger brothers or sisters, just older. Bert. Bert Shirt! No wonder he had a sad look about his eyes. That couldn't be an easy name to live with. What had his parents been thinking when they named him? And why on earth was his name in quotation marks?

The rest of the stuff was uninteresting: clothes, hankies, dull pencils, a notebook with no writing in it, cigarette papers, tobacco, two packages of ready-made cigarettes, a comb, shaving gear, an old Juicy Fruit wrapper, a package of Sen-sen, a toothbrush. I stuffed it all back into the knapsack along with the cowboy books. Then I looked at the photograph a little longer before placing it back inside the bible and the bible inside the knapsack.

There was something weird about that little boy besides his name. And those quotation marks bothered me. I wondered what Bert was doing while his family disappeared around him. Was he in Mrs. Dunning's care? I couldn't ask Jackson or he'd know I'd been snooping.

CHAPTER 9

Benny took off just one day after Jackson was released from the hospital. The garage was finished except for the paint and my dad didn't really want to pay someone for painting that he could do himself; he enjoyed painting. Benny stuck to his original plan of heading out to Alberta for the sugar beets. It was decided that he would come back for his friend in four weeks' time.

My dad gave Benny some cash and, speaking with a French-Canadian accent, wished him well. He didn't hear himself do the accent and denied it when I pointed it out. But it was something he always did. At the butcher shop he spoke like an eastern European with very good English, like Mr. Fortensky, the man behind the counter. It was a funny thing about my dad, the way he fell into another person's way of speaking. It was as though he wasn't sure where he ended and the next person began.

Jackson didn't have polio when he came home, just the two casts up past his elbows. He spent very little time in his room; he wasn't sick, after all. And he was a young man full of energy, so he mostly used his room for sleep, like the rest of us.

Sometimes I didn't think I could bear the wait until I saw him again: the overnight hours, my time at work, any few minutes when he left a room before he walked back into it again. My whole being would concentrate itself on the future moment when he would again fill my vision. My head ached with anticipation and my body squashed in on itself.

We played checkers. He told me which man to move and I moved it for him. He was good at checkers. And I read to him, mostly Thomas Hardy. He listened carefully and watched me as I read.

Unlike Benny's eyes, Jackson's seemed to shine from within. I guess it was that the light somehow entered his eyes and caught specks of gold on his irises. I couldn't figure that out, still can't, the way light changes from one set of eyes to the next.

It was a little unnerving at first, getting used to the warm light from his eyes falling all over me. But I got to like it. I prepared myself for the readings — made sure my face was shining clean in spite of my new ideas about dirt. It was easy to get a grimy face during those hot damp days when even the sun was obscured by dust. I wanted him to admire me.

We talked, too, about high school and college (he wanted a break in between the two), songs from the radio (we both liked "Summertime"), broken bones we'd had. We talked about who was a worse prime minister, Bennett or King, and about Jackson's parents. He told me that his dad had been a lot older than his mum and that he had been a big shot with the Canadian Pacific Railway. And he said that his mum should be permanently locked up in an insane asylum. Life at his home had become way harder to take after his dad had died.

"My mum no longer tries at all," he said. "She doesn't try at all."

Some of the things he told me were lies; I was sure of it. I think the lies were just to make him seem more worldly to himself and to me. He hinted at experiences with older girls and women, experiences I was almost certain he hadn't had. If it was true, why didn't he at least try to kiss me? Was I so unappealing? I would have helped.

I told him about my sister. He was interested in Sunny, in what had become of her. We speculated on that and we touched on the worst things that could happen.

He said that what was going on with him right now was pretty bad, not being able to do anything for himself and all.

That's when I told him that my mother had killed herself the summer when Sunny was kidnapped.

He turned white, as though every ounce of blood had left his head and gone south.

"That's so much worse than my broken arms, I feel embarrassed having complained about them. And you folks are being so kind to me during it all. It can't even compare."

"Don't worry," I said. "You didn't know."

Although I must say I was a little surprised that he mentioned his arms after my Sunny story. Surely Sunny's plight, in itself, was much more devastating than his paltry broken bones that were going to heal completely. I hoped that I hadn't told him about my mother in a one-upmanship kind of way. It seemed a terrible way to use her and I regretted it.

On another day, during another talk, which became more and more heated, it came out that Jackson believed that Pope Pius XI couldn't make a mistake.

I was flabbergasted. "Of course he can make mistakes," I shouted. "He's a human being."

"No, he can't!" Jackson yelled back at me.

"Yes, for the love of God, he can!"

"What's going on out there?" my dad called out the screen door to where we were sitting at the picnic table. "Keep it down, by gum!"

Jackson stuck to his guns. It upset me that he could be so stupid about this one subject.

I left him and took a walk by the river. I added it to the list of things I would discuss with Isabelle next time I saw her. Since school had let out I hadn't seen her and I missed her. She often knew the answers to things that I wondered about that I didn't want to ask Gwen or anyone else I saw regularly. Things like, is it common for Catholics to believe that the pope can't make a mistake? Isabelle wasn't a practising Catholic but she'd had lots of experience with nuns at her old school.

Aunt Helen tended to Jackson. He hated being fed, so took that over pretty quickly — sat with his face close to the table so he could wield his own fork. He used his fingers a lot — Aunt Helen thought too much — but she phoned the doctor and he said not to worry: it was good to keep them moving.

Jackson allowed me help him smoke. For some reason that didn't fall into the category of things he didn't want people to do for him. So we shared cigarettes. I was careful not to let my dad see us do that. It was deliciously intimate and I knew he'd raise a ruckus. It was that summer that I became a confirmed smoker.

We went for walks around the neighbourhood. People stared at us and asked questions. I suspected some of the busybodies thought there was something off-kilter about the situation, but I didn't care and I thought Jackson liked it. I was under the impression he enjoyed a small amount of notoriety. It turned out I was wrong about that.

I waited a few days before asking him a couple of knapsack-related questions. We were sitting in the backyard after supper and Helen and Dad were on the front verandah.

"Do you believe in God?" I asked.

"God who?" he said.

"I'm just wondering because of our Pope conversation," I said. "Do you believe in Jesus?"

"What is this?"

"Nothing. I'm just wondering."

"Well, I believe that there was a Jesus," said Jackson.

"Do you ever read the bible?"

"Violet, is this about you pillaging my knapsack?"

"What?"

"I know you went through my stuff."

"No, I didn't."

"Yes, you did."

"I did, yes," I said. There was no point in keeping it up. I would just look worse and worse the more I denied it. "How did you know?"

"My picture of Bertram was on page 200 of the bible and you stuck it back in on page 226."

"Sorry."

"You should be sorry! How would you like it if I ransacked your dresser drawers?"

I pictured my underpants, and hidden beneath them the photographs I'd cut out of magazines — shots of women whose hair looked the way I wished mine did, whose skin was smooth and flawless the way mine wasn't, and whose breasts were big and shapely the way I wanted mine to be. And worse, the diary with the broken lock that had words about Jackson on its pages.

"God, I'd hate it. I'm really sorry," I said again.

"Okay."

"Why didn't you mention it before, if you knew?" I asked.

"I don't know. I just didn't."

"You must despise me."

Jackson laughed. "Of course I don't despise you. I just think you're a little on the meddlesome side and should have your hand slapped from time to time."

He was being too nice to me. I didn't deserve it. I made a vow to myself to behave in a more grown-up manner, especially when it came to Jackson.

"Would you like some lemonade?" I asked.

"Yes, please."

When I came back with the drink I placed it carefully with a straw within his reach and sat down again.

"Is Bertram your younger brother?" I asked.

"Uh, yeah." Jackson knocked his drink over but I caught it before it spilled completely. Lemonade dripped through the boards of the picnic table onto the ground.

"Do you have any other brothers or sisters?" I asked.

"No."

"Who looks after Bertram?"

"Mrs. Dunning. My dad till he died. Me. He's in boarding school during the school year. He's at summer camp now."

"Jesuit camp?"

"No."

"Why not?"

"Lord, I don't know! You ask too many questions."

"Do other kids make fun of him?" I pressed on.

"Why would they?"

"Because his name is Bert Shirt."

"No one calls him Bert."

"Why are there quotation marks around his name?"

"What?"

"On the photograph, there are quotation marks around his name. Why?"

"I don't know."

Jackson finished what was left of his lemonade.

"Stay out of my room, okay?"

"It's not your goldarn room," I snapped. "You don't live here. This is my family's house. I'll go in there if I feel like it. I'll tear your knapsack and its stupid contents to shreds if I want to. It doesn't belong here. You don't belong here."

I stalked off. So much for my new grown-up manner.

Helen came out the back door as I went in. She was carrying Jackson's knapsack.

"What are you doing with that?" I asked.

"None of your business, Miss Nosy Parker," said Helen.

When I looked out at them from the bathroom window they were sitting companionably while Helen mended the tear in the knapsack. She would put a patch over her mending job, using her leather needle and wearing a thimble on her finger. I could hear their low voices with sudden bursts of modest laughter. They sounded like a couple.

I slipped downstairs, out the front door and over to Gwen's, where I hoped her mother wouldn't be home.

CHAPTER 10

After supper on a Friday, a week after Jackson got out of the hospital, the two of us went for a walk. I remember the date, July 10, because it was the night before the hottest day of the summer. The humidity was 100 per cent. We walked slowly up and down the dusty avenues.

"The Dionne quintuplets have a new baby brother," I said.

"Great," said Jackson.

"I read it in the paper."

"Why would they have another kid?" said Jackson. "They must be out of their minds."

We walked along without saying anything while I tried to think up another topic. Jackson never put any effort into things like topics.

"I'm glad fate conspired to bring you to us," I said and felt my face heat up. It wasn't what I meant to say. I thought I was thinking about the horses I'd heard about that had died from heat prostration.

"There's no such thing as fate," Jackson said.

"Yes, there is. Of course there is! What about when you said that you and Benny meeting up was meant to be? What about that? That's fate, isn't it?"

"Why do you pay so much attention to what I say? I didn't say that, did I?"

"Yes. You sure did."

"Well, fate isn't what brought me here."

"What, then, if not fate?"

Jackson looked at me with a crippled smile ruining his handsome face.

"Alberta sugar beets," he said. "Alberta sugar beets are what brought us to Winnipeg. We were passing through. Remember?"

"But you walked down our back lane," I said. "Our back lane! And we were out in the yard. You came to our particular street."

Jackson sighed. "Never mind, Violet."

"What? Never mind what?"

I tripped over my own feet then and saw that we were on Monck Avenue. A steady hot wind blew against us down the quiet street. I watched an eddy of dust twirl up and disappear on the sidewalk in front of Old Lady Fitzgerald's house. She was in the yard staring up at the sky.

"Hello, Mrs. Fitzgerald," I said. "It doesn't look much like rain, does it?"

"Oh, hello, Violet," she said. "No, no, I suppose not."

I introduced Jackson. She was curious about his casts so I related the story of his accident and told her that he was staying with us for a month or so.

Her bottom lip quivered. "Mercy!" she said. "Oh, my good Lord resting in his mother's arms!"

"Gosh, Mrs. Fitzgerald," I said. "It's not that bad. Aunt Helen is a nurse, remember."

As we continued along the street I smiled to myself.

"Why do you have to do that?" Jackson asked when we had turned the corner onto Kirkdale Street.

"What?"

"Use me to tease old ladies and get your thrills."

I wanted to shout out denials but I feared he was right on the mark. "She started it," I said. It was the best I could do.

"What are you thinking when you say those things?" he asked.

I felt as though he knew everything about me. All the bad things, anyway — my thoughts about his lips and his male member. I wasn't sure there was anything good to know about me.

Without giving it any thought, I took off running. My sandals were no good for this. But I ran anyway, all the way down Claremont to the river. I didn't want to see him again so I turned left. I couldn't run anymore — I was seriously puffed out — but I walked along the riverbank to a spot I knew across from the icehouse and sat down in the stinkweed and the wild asparagus that had been picked clean.

The pink sun was going down behind clouds of softly coloured dust, orangey-tan. It was a beautiful sight, but I was in no mood for beauty. And it was hard not to think about that dust as earth under someone's wornout shoes in Saskatchewan, about their soil and livelihood blowing out from under them. I didn't have room for those kinds of thoughts.

The icehouse was locked up for the night. I wished I had a small clean chunk to suck on.

I believed that Satan had a hold on me and that's what made me so bad. No amount of Aunt Helen telling me that the devil was nonsense would convince me otherwise. She found it particularly absurd that I had such a shaky hold on God but didn't question the existence of Satan.

The deep lines under my eyes that I'd had since I was a kid were his outward manifestation. I truly believed that. They cut my face in half in what I saw as a sinister way.

When I'd asked Helen what those lines meant, she'd said, "They're just little dents, honey. Nothing to worry about." She'd peered into my face. "I can hardly see them."

She didn't know.

I tried to read about Satan but it was like reading about God. It was like trying to peel invisible potatoes.

Sometimes I thought it must be connected to my sister, Sunny, this feeling I had of being close to the devil. I came so near to the worst evil in the world on the day she was taken. I breathed in vile black air and it never left me. It found a good fit.

It was in the days after my mother's death that I first found those grooves underneath my eyes. I was just six years old.

The world was covered in a brown wash now, worse than dust. Why couldn't I just have talked about dead horses to Jackson? Why did I have to show him the pathetic inside of me?

I felt a nameless free-floating fear. I thought about walking over to the St. Boniface Cathedral to talk to a priest. You go into a little booth like with Madame Cora at the Casey Shows. But the confessionals are much more elegant than Madame Cora's booth, with its stink of Green Wind perfume and her little cigars. You always came out of Cora's booth feeling sticky and desolate no matter what she said.

Gwen and I went to mass at the cathedral one morning during a summer that was cooler than this one, just to see. That's how I knew what it was like there. Gwen was an Anglican and she went to St. Phillips when she did go, which wasn't very often. She was worse than me in lots of things.

We even took communion that sweat-free day at the cathedral, ate wafers and drank wine and made grunting sounds when we received them, in an effort to behave like everyone else. We found out later that they had been saying "amen."

Norwood United Church, where I belonged, didn't seem quite so steeped in God and the devil. There was no incense there or Latin; we didn't even drink real wine at communion. What good was that?

Maybe, I thought, I could go into a confessional now and talk to a priest about my ties to Satan. Would he understand and try to help me? I could ask him his beliefs on whether or not the pope could make a mistake. I knew what his answer would be and I didn't want to know. Visiting the Catholic church no longer seemed like a good idea.

Evening turned to night and the murky shadows saw me home. The worst that could happen was that Jackson would be gone and I'd never see him again. I knew there were far worse things — my dad could be dead from a stroke, our house could be on fire, I could wake up tomorrow with polio — but right now they paled next to the thought of never seeing Jackson Shirt again.

Helen and my dad were in the front room. My dad was reading the book of Bertrand Russell essays that Mr. Larkin had lent him and Helen was crocheting a winter hat for a kid — a rural kid who would otherwise freeze his ears in the coming winter. She knitted or crocheted whatever the church ladies told her was most needed. She wasn't much of a churchgoer herself but she did all kinds of good church-like things, unlike Gert Walker, who was a regular at St. Phillips, but hadn't done a good deed in her life except not aborting her two children who turned out to be friends of mine.

Sometimes I envied Gwen her little brother, even though she had to look after him sometimes. He didn't really need much looking after — he was so self-sufficient — pretty much all you could hope for in a younger sibling. I hoped his mother wouldn't ruin him.

"How's Gwen?" Helen asked.

"Oh! She's good," I said, wondering where that came from.

"Jackson told us that was where he thought you were going when you abandoned him," said my dad. "To Gwen's house."

"I didn't abandon him! Did he say that?"

"No. Those were my words."

My dad was warming to Jackson in his weakened state. I guess he saw him as less of a threat to my virtue since his casts made it impossible for him to manhandle me unless I placed various parts of myself in his hands, which would be extremely difficult and take far more gumption than I possessed. It made an unsightly picture in my head, unlike the soft kisses I imagined and which involved only our sweet clean faces.

"Where is he?" I asked.

"In his room," said Helen. "Did you two have a tiff?"

"No! Jesus!" I said. "What would we have a tiff about? We don't have tiffs."

"Don't say *Jesus*," said my dad.

I rolled my eyes.

"Don't roll your eyes," he said. "They'll stay that way."

I laughed and kissed them both goodnight, something I hadn't done in a while. When I leaned over to kiss Dad's cheek I saw that the essay he was reading was titled "Why I Am Not a Christian."

Jackson had made up a story about my going to Gwen's house and I was grateful for that. He hadn't told on me for running away from him.

"Fraser Foote phoned," Helen called after me.

"What did he want?" I asked, trying to sound casual.

"I don't know. He said he'd call back tomorrow. He probably wants to begin a course of sweeping you off your feet."

My dad chuckled.

I hoped Jackson could hear this conversation from his room and think that I was much sought after.

CHAPTER 11

That was the hottest weekend of the summer. I slept very little that Friday night, tossing and turning under a twisted sheet, in and out of my polio dreams: my hands were unable to grasp a fork or use the telephone, my legs gave way and by the time I dragged myself to the chesterfield I couldn't turn my head from side to side. My eyes closed and I couldn't open them again or my lips to speak.

When I awoke, the sheets were soaking wet. I looked at my alarm clock — 5:20. Four hours at the very outside till I would see Jackson again. I couldn't imagine waiting that long. I didn't care about our tiff, as Helen called it, and I didn't think he cared either. He was just playing with me. He loved me too, I knew it. How could someone I loved so much not love me back in the same way? It didn't seem possible. I'd read about unrequited love, but I was pretty sure it wasn't for me.

I must have dozed off again because the time passed somehow. At 8:30 I dragged myself out of my damp nest with its paralyzing dreams and headed to the bathroom. In a matter of minutes I would be seeing him, in less than the length of an *Amos and Andy* show for sure. I could handle that; I could fill that time.

As I passed Jackson's room I heard a muffled groan. I stopped and listened for more but there was only silence for the next few moments. The hardwood creaked beneath my bare feet as I resumed my short trek to the bathroom. I worried that Jackson would think I'd been eavesdropping on him. His door opened then and Aunt Helen came out. She carried a basin of water and when she saw me a little of it sloshed out onto the floor.

"Dadgummit!" she said. "Violet! What are you doing, standing there like a sentry?" She flushed an ugly pink colour to the roots of her salt-and-pepper hair.

"Nothing. I'm just on my way to the bathroom."

"Why aren't you at work?"

"Because it's Saturday."

"Oh! Oh, yes."

"What were you doing in there?" I asked.

"Giving Jackson a sponge bath."

"What else were you doing?"

"Nothing."

"I don't believe you. Why are you flustered?"

She pushed her way past me into the bathroom, slopping more water onto the floor and finally pouring the rest of it down the bathtub drain.

I followed her down to the kitchen.

Aunt Helen rinsed out the basin in the kitchen sink and turned it upside down on the draining board.

"He was horribly engorged," she said quietly. She put her hand beside her mouth and whispered, "It looked positively painful."

"So what did you do?"

She opened the fridge door and reached for a tray of eggs. "I must speak to the egg man," she said. "I had to throw away four eggs this week. They had a funny smell. I wonder what he feeds those hens of his."

"What did you do?" I said again.

"Oh, Violet." Helen set the eggs down and looked at me. "If you must know, I hit it with a pencil first and that didn't work. Poor Jackson was embarrassed so I took care of it for him."

"So it was your duty as a nurse?"

"Don't be ignorant!"

"Well?"

"Violet, there was nothing sexual about it. It's something we did all the time for the boys in the war."

During Helen's tour of duty overseas much of her work had been in field hospitals and she'd won commendations for her bravery. Apparently she had also vigorously rubbed the swollen members of soldiers who were unable to do it for themselves. She was a practised masturbator of others.

"We?" I said.

"Yes. The other nurses and I."

"Grace Box?"

"Perhaps. You'll have to be sure to ask her next time you see her."

"Are you sure it wasn't just you?" I asked. "Did your supervisor know what you were up to?"

"Oh, I see. You're planning on reporting me, are you? Go and have your bath, Violet. You're making me very angry. You shouldn't be talking to me this way. I'm your aunt."

"Aunt be darned!" I said. "Nurse be darned! What if it happens again tomorrow? What if he's embarrassed again tomorrow? Will you do him again?"

"Don't be crude, Violet." Helen began cracking eggs into a bowl and cutting thick slices of her homemade bread.

"Hah!" I said.

She threw a wet rag at me as I turned to leave the room.

"No breakfast for me, thanks," I said and trudged back up the stairs. I took care of the puddles of water in the upstairs hall. I was pretty sure no one wanted Jackson taking a dive on a slippery floor and breaking a leg.

"I could use some help after you're freshened up," Helen called after me.

"Fat chance," I muttered.

I couldn't erase the picture in my head of my aunt with an engorged appendage in one hand and a small towel in the other waiting to catch the semen of soldiers. And of Jackson! I'd have thrown up if I'd had any food in my guts.

He came out of his room as I was kicking a wall in the hallway. I hurt my toes.

"Easy there," he said.

I couldn't look at him.

"Is your foot okay?"

I could hear the concern in his voice but I didn't believe it.

"Never mind me, how about you? Is your male member okay?" I wanted to say, but all I did say was, "No," as I closed the bathroom door behind me.

I wondered if Jackson suspected that I knew. He must have. Did he even care? I felt ugly and gawky and sweat-covered and I hated the face I saw in the mirror. He hadn't been mocking or crude or superior or any of the things I imagined he might be after being rubbed to satisfaction by my aunt. He was just his regular self.

They hadn't done it to hurt me. What they had done had nothing to do with me at all. But still, it worsened the feelings I still had from the night before, from remembering the pictures I knew Jackson had seen inside my head.

I cleaned the tub to rid it of the last of the Jackson slime that Helen had flushed away. He was no better than me, no purer than me. Neither was Helen. What they had done made me feel like garbage, like the four foul eggs Helen had thrown out. Why was that, when it had nothing to do with me?

How many times had this happened between Jackson and Helen? There was no way now that I could ask her. My attitude had taken care of that. I wondered if his member was big, medium, or small. I couldn't ask her that, either. She was mad at me and I was…I don't know what I was — it kept changing. I was curious; that's for sure. I wondered for a second if she'd let me assist in her ministrations. Not a chance. Not even if she wasn't angry. Too bad — I figured I'd be good at it with a little guidance. I had good strong hands, my dad often said, but I doubt if he associated their strength with the gripping of male organs.

Helen couldn't be totally at ease with what she had done or she wouldn't have been so flustered when she saw me in the hall. I decided to apologize. Cool as a cucumber, I would be. She would forgive me. Aunt Helen was the forgiving type.

I ran a full tub and sprinkled lavender scent into the water. I wanted to slip through one of Benny's holes in the atmosphere and sit by a cool mountain stream in 1878 where there were no Jacksons or Helens or erect members. I wanted to push my fresh clean self through the mire of their filth and triumph over their wicked ways from a faraway place.

When I glanced out the bathroom window I saw my dad admiring his new garage. It still needed paint but it looked good. A small smile relaxed his face.

"Good job!" I called out the window. Cool as a cucumber, that was me.

He looked up and laughed. "Not bad, eh?"

If he knew what had just gone on in the upstairs of his house he would have had a massive stroke and died for sure.

I had a leisurely bath, lingering in the tub. I decided to take small advantage of my spat with Helen to let breakfast go by without pitching in, let Helen sweat thinking of something to tell my dad about my absence.

Jealousy burned underneath my idea of how cool I was. A cool mess. No amount of bathing was going to clean me. I was sure that Helen thought she was telling the truth about it not being a sexual thing. I didn't believe it for a minute, but I was certain that she did.

Later that day, as I sat at the kitchen table snipping the ends off green beans with the kitchen scissors, I said, "I'm sorry, Helen, that I behaved badly this morning."

She didn't turn from the sink where she was scrubbing the dirt from new potatoes.

"Apology accepted," she announced briskly.

I couldn't think of anything else to say, so that's how we left it, even though to me it felt unfinished. I thought she could have admitted out loud to some sort of transgressive behaviour to even things out a little more between us, but the admission never came.

CHAPTER 12

On that Saturday, July 11th, the temperature reached 108 degrees Fahrenheit, an all-time record. People were dying every day, mostly older folks. The day before, the Friday, a nine-year-old Norwood boy had died of a heart attack at Winnipeg Beach. I didn't know him. He lived on the other side of St. Mary's Road. But I think that Saturday was the worst day for dying. We hadn't had a day under 90 for over a week.

Isabelle came and called on me that night. I introduced her to Dad and Helen and Jackson, who were all sitting on the verandah.

"Hi," she said. She nodded at Jackson. "I've heard about you."

We all laughed, a bit nervously

"Yeah, I'm famous," he said, and we laughed a little more.

Isabelle and I went up to my room and she convinced me that we should go for a swim in the Red River. I was hesitant, never having done it before.

"I can't believe that," she said. "How could you live so close to the river and never have swum in it? That's what it's there for."

Just sixteen, Isabelle was several months younger than me, but she seemed older, not to look at — she was just a little bit of a thing — but she knew stuff: she knew where the lady bookie lived, she knew where to get booze if you didn't care how good it tasted, she had seen a dick, as she called it, before she turned seven, one that hadn't belonged to her dad or brother. Stuff like that. I admired her.

Dick was a good word for it. I decided to adopt it.

Isabelle had transferred in to our school last fall from one that was run by nuns. Isabelle had a thing about nuns; she didn't like them. That was the first thing she ever said to me: I don't like nuns.

"Why?" I had asked.

"Because they made my knuckles swell and my ears ring." She'd rubbed one hand over the knuckles on the other.

In June she had told me that that year, grade eleven, was her last at school. She had to quit to help support her family.

"Oh no," I'd said. "You have to go back in the fall."

"Can't," she said.

"You have to."

"Can't," she said again and that had been that.

I hadn't seen her since that conversation in June.

"So did you find a job?" I asked now as we made our way in the quickening dark down Lyndale Drive toward the rowing club.

"Yeah, I work as a courier," Isabelle said. "I use my bike and go to different offices downtown."

"That sounds all right," I said.

"Yeah, you hear lots of gossip when you deal with so many people in a day," she said. "It can be kind of fun. That's how I heard about the guy with the two casts."

"Jackson."

"Yeah."

"Really?'

"Really."

"Gee whiz, news really travels."

"Yup."

"What exactly did you hear about him?"

"Just that some punk hobo fell off a roof in the Flats, broke both his arms and was staying with a family here, right inside their house. I didn't know it was your family."

"He's not a punk hobo," I said. "He was educated by Jesuits."

Isabelle laughed. "I'll pass that on."

"Please do."

I don't know why I defended him. I wanted to tell Isabelle about what my aunt had done but the words caught in my throat. Another day, perhaps, when it had had more time to settle.

Instead I told her about my job at Eaton's and the nutty letters I had to answer.

"Sitting at a desk would be hard for me," she said. "Too much like school. God, I hated school!"

Soon we were standing on the dock at the rowing club with our bathing costumes under our clothes. I had told Dad and Helen that I was walking Isabelle partway home.

I couldn't find the moon or even one star behind the clouds and dust. The river was low and black and almost quiet. The smell was wet and good — the same as always. Helen would disagree; she thought the river stunk of unmentionable things. Just for fun I used to try to get her to mention them but she never would.

Isabelle sat down and took off her sneakers. I did the same. Then we took off our damp clothes and laid them on the dock. I tried the water with the toes of one foot. Warmish cool. I was worried about the certain filth, Helen's unmentionables, but kept it to myself. I didn't want Isabelle to think I was squeamish; she was so doggone brave.

"Don't dive," said Isabelle. "You never know what's in there."

I was sweating from fear as much as from the hot night air but I followed her into the water, slipping in feet first and pushing out from the wooden dock. I very much didn't want to touch the bottom.

"Can you feel the current?" asked Isabelle.

"Yeah, but it's okay." I'd been worried about that, too. You heard so much about the swift current of the Red and how it sweeps you away before you know it.

"It's not so strong when the water's low like this from no rain," Isabelle said. "But there are always swirling eddies near the bridge. We won't swim too close to it."

I'm a strong swimmer. My dad taught me on excursions to Lake Winnipeg since as far back as when my mum was alive. One of my favourite memories is learning to float. I can't remember his instructions, but whatever they were they worked. One moment I was flailing about, all frantic arms and legs, and the next I was calm, riding the gentle movement of the lake, face down in gladness.

"Look," said Isabelle and pointed toward the dock.

Two dark forms moved about in the vicinity of our clothes.

"It's the Willis brothers," said Isabelle.

"Stay away from our clothes, creeps!" she shouted.

I heard a high-pitched giggle, almost girlish.

"There's someone else with them," Isabelle said. "There's three of them."

"I only see two," I said.

"It's that ugly Botham guy."

"Dirk? No, it couldn't be," I said. "What would he be doing hanging around with the Willises?"

"It's him all right," said Isabelle."

"Unh-uh, no way," I said. "You think Dirk is ugly?"

"Ugleee," shouted Isabelle.

I didn't have much hope for our clothes.

We swam out into the middle of the river. I did the breaststroke mostly and the sidestroke, not keen on losing my face in the water. I wasn't comfortable enough to give myself up to the experience like Isabelle, who dove under and came up yards away, did the butterfly, hooted quietly as she did the back crawl. She positively frolicked.

There was moving silver on the water from the lamplight and vehicles on the Norwood Bridge. It looked like the liquid mercury we had messed around with in the chemistry lab last term. I kept the dolphin movements of my friend in sight as I swam steadily toward the far shore. The current was slight and I gradually surrendered to the water and felt as though I could swim forever.

When I reached the other side I clambered up the bank, grasping hold of the sturdy stems of weeds. It felt like wild rhubarb, overlooked by tramps and wives scouring the banks for something to round out their evening meals.

Isabelle was more puffed out than me, her energy depleted by her playfulness.

We laughed for a while at nothing in particular.

"Let's walk back over the bridge," Isabelle said when she caught her breath. "I'm too exhausted to swim anymore."

I could have swum Lake Winnipeg that night but I didn't want to go alone so I climbed alongside her up to the bridge, stepping on thistles and sharp stones all the way. Shouts and wolf whistles bounced off us as we crossed the bridge. Finally we reached the dock and our shoes; at least they had left us our shoes.

That night it didn't drop below 82 degrees and on Sunday we were back up to 104. In the morning I walked back to the rowing club to look for our clothes in the light of day. They were hidden in some bushes not far out of sight. Good. Stupid boys! Then I saw that they had been torn to shreds. Not so good. Some of the cuts were so clean I knew they had used knives. I didn't like knives.

I looked out across the brown river to where the water met the dried gumbo on the other side, several feet of it, above the water line, naked in the sun. It shouldn't have been that way. The water yielded to the land far too soon. I knew that I would never swim in the river again; it had been a one and only thing.

It hadn't occurred to me that the boys would destroy our clothes. I had thought the worst that could happen was that they would hide them or maybe take them away so that we'd never find them. This was past being mean and it scared me.

Surely it couldn't have been Dirk with the Willises. Gwen couldn't be in love with a knife-wielding maniac. I was pretty certain that Isabelle was mistaken about that. I picked up all our clothes and took them home. It wasn't clear to me what I would do with them or even if I would tell Isabelle about it, but I wanted to put our shorts and shirts somewhere safe. I stuffed them into a brown paper bag and stashed it in the back of my closet.

Fraser Foote phoned me on Sunday afternoon and we made a date for the following Friday.

CHAPTER 13

Clouds drifted around all day on Monday, tantalizing dark clouds that promised more than dust. I stared out the window on the far side of the office and thought about the rain that hadn't fallen yet. When I left the mail-order building at five o'clock, the temperature felt downright cool. Someone said it had dropped fifteen degrees in three hours. The wind was fierce and on my short walk to the streetcar I held my head down against the driving uptown dirt. I started to run when the thunder began. It was so close it felt like it was inside of me tearing me up like a crazed fetus.

"Please don't let lightning strike my house," I said out loud, "or me, or anyone. Don't let it strike that horrid Jackson Shirt."

I didn't make it home before the rain came, but I did make it onto the streetcar. When we got over the Norwood Bridge the driver stopped to wait out the torrential downpour. It didn't last long, maybe half an hour, but a huge amount of rain fell. Sirens screamed from every direction. They sounded like they came from a giant firehouse in the sky.

"Good luck!" the driver said when he let me off at Walmer Street and Claremont, by the Buena Vista Court.

I took off my shoes and stockings; under the circumstances I didn't care who saw me. My sandals were new and my stockings pure silk with no snags so far; I didn't want to ruin them.

A tree and a hydro pole were down at the corner of Walmer and Lawndale. A small crowd of boys and mothers had gathered round to stare. The dads, like me, were making their way home from work. The streets were mud soup on my trek home. Even where gravel had been laid the dirt won out.

Jackson's casts would have washed away in a rain like that; I was glad the loathsome beggar had a roof over his head.

He and my dad and Aunt Helen were out in the front yard surveying the damage when I trudged up with my shoes in my hand. The sun was already trying to poke through as the fast-moving clouds shifted and then covered it again. I saw an invisible spidery thread, impervious to catastrophe, joining Helen and Jackson through branches and air currents.

"Thank God you're home," Helen said when she saw me.

"Violet!" said my dad.

I swear, I don't think he realized I was out in all that weather.

"Go in and change your clothes, honey," he said. "You're soaking wet."

I looked down at my drenched self. My brassiere and garter belt were clearly defined beneath my flimsy summer dress and slip. All my small curves and tiny bumps showed themselves through the sodden material.

They all stared; Helen stared the worst. My dad looked away as I started toward the steps.

"If it was any less than two inches of rain that fell I'll eat my hat," he said as he piled fallen branches to one side of the yard.

"I'll turn on the radio and see how the rest of the city's coping," I said.

"The power's out," Jackson and Helen said together.

I barrelled into their spidery thread to get to the house. It didn't stop me but it didn't break either — just stretched and stretched.

Upstairs, I looked in my full-length mirror and saw what the others had seen. I didn't care. I cared that my dad saw, but not the other two. I knew that if I were compared naked to Aunt Helen in any contest, anywhere, I would win. Unless the contest was for most matronly figure or lowest hanging breasts.

I pictured Aunt Helen at the top of the Ferris wheel at the Casey Shows. I watched her lean over to wave at someone far far below. She toppled clear out of her seat and fell end over flowery end into the complicated machinery of the rickety old ride. Maybe she had been waving at Jackson and now he was left to pull her twisted body from the wreckage. Her arm came off in his hand. And he was horrified to see that her head was no longer attached to her body. He ran screaming from the scene into the path of a pair of runaway horses and met his own bloody end.

It was eerie how the inside of me transformed without my being aware of it, changed over short time periods like the combined liquids in my Petri dish in chemistry class. These altered feelings toward Jackson and Helen tripped me up far more than any experiment in that unfathomable laboratory.

I put on new underwear and a clean but well-worn sundress that I wore for working around the house and yard. After throwing my wet clothes into the bathtub I towelled my hair and looked out my bedroom window at the destruction.

Thank goodness for my dad. If it weren't for him I wouldn't have known where or who to be. His befuddlement at watching me walk out of the aftermath of the storm and his dismay at my see-through clothes were typical Dad behaviour and I savoured it. It was normal, unlike so many other things going on around there. I would have appreciated a bit more concern for my well-being as opposed to my transparent clothes, but I supposed I hadn't been in any real danger.

Back downstairs, I tried the radio. The power was still off. I helped my dad with branches while Helen went inside to fix supper. I didn't know where Jackson was, but he was out of the way of my dad and me.

The four of us ate at the kitchen table. It was a subdued supper; my dad did most of the talking — about the storm and the destruction and the state of the roads and how he was going to eat his hat. His ignorance of what had occurred between Helen and Jackson saved us. The three of us could manage it. The four of us wouldn't have had a chance.

After supper we ate ice cream on the front verandah in the silver afterlight of the rain. A car drove by and raised no dust. Warren, Gwen's little brother, came along with his dog, Tippy.

"Anything I can help you folks with?" he asked.

He had his red Super-Streak wagon with him. He and his wagon and his dog were covered in mud from stem to stern. His slingshot stuck out of the back pocket of his trousers. At the ready.

"Thanks a lot, Warren," said my dad. "I think we've got things pretty well under control here. We didn't get hit as badly as some."

"Would you like some ice cream?" asked Helen.

"Yes, please!" said Warren. "Ma'am," he added, a little late.

The Walkers had to watch every penny, so ice cream didn't turn up often at their table. They were more likely to have bread pudding or many times nothing at all.

I went to get him a bowl of Neapolitan and he sat in his wagon to eat it so we didn't have to tell him that he was too filthy to come inside, even as far as the verandah. When he was done he left a little in the bowl for his dog to finish up.

Tippy was the best dog, a quiet dog. She never barked. She was so smart you'd swear there was more going on in her head than regular canine thoughts. She was a mongrel, a cross between a collie and something that didn't have a pointed nose.

"Thanks kindly," Warren said and set his bowl on the top step. So long, now."

"So long, Warren," we called out, one big happy family.

"I wish Warren belonged to us," I said and then I wished I hadn't when I saw the look on my dad's face.

Sunny rarely came up, all these years later. It wasn't like with Gwen's dad — we were allowed to talk about her — we just didn't. But she hung in the moist air now, hovered at about chest level for a few moments.

"He's a good little fella," Dad said, breaking the silence. "I like him, too."

"No one deserves Gert Walker for a mum," I said.

"She couldn't be all bad if Gwen and Warren have turned out as well as they have," said my dad.

"Gwen's not so great," I said.

"Violet, she's your best chum!" said Helen.

"Actually, I don't think she is," I said. "I think I'm starting to prefer Isabelle."

"Honestly!" said Helen. "The fickleness of youth!"

"Yeah, well, that's me," I said. "Youthful. Fickle. It could be worse. I could be a nymphomaniac."

I don't know why I said it; I hadn't realized I was going to. Maybe it was the small sense of well-being I felt in the aftermath of the storm: we had all survived, had we not?

My dad's mouth opened after I said it, but no words came out. Maybe he thought he misheard me. Helen stood up and ordered me to help her carry our empty dishes into the house. Major Helen. Jackson laughed out loud for just a second, an abrupt, heh! and then stopped himself.

It turned out it was more like one and a half inches of rain that fell so we teased my dad the next day about which hat he was going to eat.

"I think it should be your winter hat with the ear flaps," said Helen. "Now that's what I call a hat!"

Even Jackson joined in. "I think your straw hat might be the easiest to digest," he said.

My dad laughed.

That day was as hot as Hades after the sun came up, but after that there was a break in the heat for a few days.

One person had been struck by lightning during the storm, a man from Ile des Chenes. We read about it in the paper.

Norwood got off easy compared to some sections of the city. St. James and Fort Garry were the worst hit. There were roofs blown off buildings, windows smashed and power lines down all over the place. A streetcar burned on Logan Avenue when wires fell down on top of it.

A few downed branches and a little seepage in the basement where an eave fell away from the house were hardly worth mentioning compared to having your roof blown off.

CHAPTER 14

On Friday evening I went to the Met with Fraser Foote to see *Private Number* starring Robert Taylor and Loretta Young. It was pretty good, but I was nervous about being on an actual date. My palms felt clammy and I was terrified that he would try to hold my hand. He didn't. All that worry for nothing.

Afterwards we went to Picardy's — not the one where we'd been the day that Sunny was stolen — I had never been back there. This was another Picardy's, further west down Portage Avenue. I had a cherry soda and Fraser had a vanilla milkshake.

"What's with those men hanging around your house all summer?" he asked.

"How do you mean, what's with them?"

"Well, isn't it kind of unusual?"

"No."

What was this? Fraser was supposed to be nice and he was supposed to be sweet on me.

"They helped my dad build his garage," I said, "and one of them broke his arms and...you know all this stuff, Fraser, everybody does. And one of them is gone now. It's just the man with the broken arms who's still here."

"Why is he still here?"

I sighed. "Because he broke both his arms so he needs help. Not that it's any of your business."

"Sorry. It isn't, is it? Dirk asked me to ask you about him."

"Dirk Botham?"

"Yeah."

"Dirk's a gink."

"I know," Fraser said. "Why does Gwen go out with him?"

"Because she's cuckoo. Why do you hang around with him?"

"I don't know. I'm cuckoo too, I guess." He laughed. "Besides, I don't really hang around with him unless I have to."

"Why would you have to?"

"Well, sometimes he just won't go away. I think he likes the fact that my dad's a cop. He wants to talk about police stuff with him."

"What kind of police stuff?"

"I don't know. My dad won't give him the time of day. He thinks he wears his pants pulled up too high."

We both laughed at that and I said that I agreed with his dad.

Fraser finished his shake, careful not to make slurping sounds at the end.

"Does Dirk ever hang out with the Willis brothers?" I asked.

"Not that I know of," said Fraser. "Why?"

"Oh…nothing," I said. I could see him eyeing my soda. There was more than half of it still left in the glass.

"Anyway," he said, "when my dad heard I was going to see you tonight he asked me to find out if there was any chance one of those men would still be interested in building him a new shed."

"Really?"

"Yeah."

"Well, that's great. I mean Benny is gone, like I said, but he's coming back for Jackson. So I'm sure it could happen. But not for a couple of weeks at least."

"You're on a first-name basis with these guys?" Fraser said.

"Is that another Dirk-related comment?" I asked.

He smiled. "No. Sorry. I think that was me talking."

"Is this shed thing happening because I went over to your house a few weeks ago and tried to talk your dad into it?"

"Did you do that?"

"Yeah. Didn't he mention it?"

"No. What he did mention was that your aunt came over and talked to my mum."

"What!"

"She convinced my mum to get my dad to hire one of the men. I overheard them talking."

"When was this?"

"A while back. I don't know. It must have been before the guy broke his arms."

I had mentioned my visit with Mr. Foote to Helen. She must have taken the ball and run with it. I'd had no idea.

"Why would she do that?" I knew my face was red. Did the whole world know that my elderly aunt had a crush on a seventeen-year-old boy?

"Because times are hard," Fraser said, "and people are starving and we're not and she's a good person."

"Yeah, I guess." I pushed my soda away. Helen couldn't stand the thought of Jackson leaving town so she'd tried to line up more work. Then he'd broken his arms. She'd be pleased with this new development, I thought. If Benny had work, maybe Jackson would stay with him and she wouldn't have to say goodbye for another clump of the summer. I knew I was right. Good person be darned!

"Aren't you going to drink that?" Fraser asked.

"No, go ahead." I pushed the drink closer to him and he wolfed it down in one go.

"God, they make good stuff here," he said.

Fraser was pretty sure his dad wouldn't care when work on the shed began since he hadn't even planned on it till my aunt and I and then Mrs. Foote started pestering him. He was probably just doing it because of the promise he made to my dad all those years ago about finding Sunny. Maybe he felt guilty about his failure.

My dad never forgot how kind Mr. Foote had been during that time and he was pleased that I had a date with Fraser.

"He's a fine lad," Dad had said, even though he barely knew him.

When the time came for Fraser to leave me at my door that night he tried to kiss me on the mouth, but I turned my head away and his lips brushed lightly against my ear. It felt pretty good to me, but I knew he was disappointed.

CHAPTER 15

Four weeks after the accident Jackson's doctor cut off the cast on his right arm and replaced it with one that stopped below his elbow. He could bend his arm now. There was an ugly scab inside his elbow where he had scratched at it with an unwound wire hanger. I hadn't seen him do it, but he must have done it a lot because the injury was nasty. Aunt Helen dressed it and scolded him.

On the evening of the day the cast came off we all went to a show at the Capitol Theatre. Helen figured a celebration was warranted. Jackson got to pick the show and he chose *Poppy*, starring W.C. Fields, with *The Case Against Mrs. Ames* as the second feature. I was disappointed; *Hands Across the Table* was playing at the Province and I wanted to see it. It starred Carole Lombard and she was my favourite actress. I thought W.C. Fields was creepy, what I'd seen of him. I wished I could stay home but I had invited Gwen and she asked if she could bring Dirk and it was out of control.

Dirk avoided me, but that was nothing new. Anyway, it was not the time to confront him about his Willis-related activities. I wished I had invited Fraser, but it was too late now.

We piled into the Buick: my dad and I, Aunt Helen, Jackson, Gwen, Dirk Botham, and Mr. Larkin, who decided to come at the last minute.

"The more the merrier," said my dad.

If he was using his car he liked it to be full of people. It seemed wasteful to him if every last inch of available space wasn't taken up.

I was long past worrying about Gwen stealing Jackson away from me. It no longer applied to the situation: Gwen was in love with Dirk and had eyes for no one else. To my mind, Helen loomed as the larger threat, unpleasant as that was to digest. Besides, I wished for Jackson to be trampled by runaway horses and my mild interest in Fraser Foote was growing.

Gwen found the whole Jackson situation distasteful. I could feel her judgments on our family trickling down from her mother, who pretended to be very straightlaced. They would no more have had an armless transient staying in their home than a common prostitute, although I knew Gert was a fallen woman at heart; I just knew it.

The previous Sunday I'd heard her tell Warren to stay away from our house. She didn't know I was in their backyard. I guess she figured Gwen was old enough to keep herself from getting sucked into the vortex of evil at our place, but Warren was still a little boy. I pretended I didn't hear. Warren saw me and didn't answer his mum. The little guy looked like he wanted to run. I made an about-turn and went home before I had even seen Gwen. I didn't mention it to my dad, but I told Aunt Helen.

"Gert Walker is ignorant," she said. "You needn't pay any attention to what she says. Unclench your fists, Violet."

"Tippy doesn't even like her," I said.

"Well, there you are then."

And we'd left it at that.

When I'd mentioned to Gwen on a previous occasion that her mum didn't seem all that fond of me, she denied it vehemently. The most I could get out of her was that the disappearance of my baby sister, Sunny, had hit her very hard at the time.

"Harder than it hit us?" I asked.

"Of course not!" said Gwen.

"Did she even know us then?" I asked. "You didn't move here till grade three."

"We lived on Tremblay Street. It's not that far. News like that travels fast."

She said it in the same way her mother would have said it, as if Sunny's disappearance was a disgrace to our family, like when infants

die in their cribs for no apparent reason. The families of those babies
are forever looked at askance.

"You shouldn't have told me that," I said.

"Well, you asked me," said Gwen.

"Still, you shouldn't have."

Gert Walker and others like her blamed my mother for the
loss of our Sunny. They thought our family didn't know how to be,
that it didn't know how to keep itself safe, possibly even that danger
emanated from us and infected those who came near.

My lips began to tremble and my eyes filled with tears so I ran
off home. I didn't want to cry on Walker territory. Gwen called out
after me but she didn't follow.

I decided that day not to waste any more good behaviour on
Gert Walker.

Anyway, the seven of us headed downtown squashed inside
the Buick, three in the front, four in the back. Gwen sat on Dirk's
lap. Ugh.

At the theatre we sat in a row: my dad, Mr. Larkin, Dirk,
Gwen, me, Jackson, and Aunt Helen. It wasn't the seating
arrangement I would have chosen, but I got swept along. The
show wasn't my cup of tea, but it seemed to agree with all the
others. It was hard for me to picture sitting there through the
second feature so I tried not to think about it. I ate popcorn
and tried to chew quietly so that Jackson, the punk hobo,
wouldn't hear me. I had grown to enjoy Isabelle's description of
him and I was waiting for a chance to call him that to his face.
Or at least to Helen's face.

Every now and then when he shifted, his leg would touch mine
but he would jerk it away quickly as though I were made of hot
embers. His left arm with the big cast was beside me. He set it on
the armrest after checking with me to make sure it was okay. His
right arm, the one that he could now bend, the one with the festering
sore, was on Helen's side.

I couldn't get comfortable. The seating was all wrong. If I had
choreographed it, Helen wouldn't be seated next to Jackson and

neither would I. I tried to concentrate on the show. The jokes seemed stupid to me.

To my left everything felt close to normal: Gwen adoring the gink, Mr. Larkin and my dad, clean and good, laughing their fool heads off. Apparently W.C. Fields was very much to their tastes.

To my right, Jackson was chewing gum with his mouth open. I didn't want Gwen to hear him. She thought little enough of him as it was. I felt a tension as his chewing stopped and I worried just as much about that. Had he seen inside my head again? I glanced at him and then quickly back to the screen. It could have been explained away as a neck adjustment. He caught the glance; I saw him catch it with his unsmiling face. The audience roared at that point, the biggest laugh so far. Everyone joined in except Jackson and me. Helen's loud trill pierced my right ear and I wanted to slit her throat.

Worse, Dirk giggled. When I heard that sound I knew it had been him there that night, that he'd had a hand in slashing my clothes to bits, mine and Isabelle's. No two males of the species could sound like that when they laughed.

To my left, Gwen snorted and put her hand over her mouth and nose in embarrassment. I wished for a moment that I were eleven years old hunting for golf balls with my friend who didn't believe that her evil boyfriend was good and that her best girlfriend came from a suspect family. I knew she wouldn't listen to anything bad I had to tell her about Dirk; I wasn't sure I'd even try.

It was a sunny day where W.C. Fields lived and the bright white screen shone down on the audience. When I looked past Gwen at Dirk he turned his head toward me and made a gross lizardy motion with his tongue. That reptilian tongue was the ugliest thing I'd ever seen, the way it wriggled its pointed shape in my direction. I needed to get out of there. I concentrated on the screen, determined not to look again to my left or right.

Promptly I looked to my right and saw what I had been set on not seeing. Aunt Helen's left arm was by her side, her fingers poking out past the armrest. Those fingers rested silently on top of Jackson's, her hand dark against his bright new cast. They weren't holding hands. The cast prevented that. The scene had a protective look to it, but still, my guts churned. It didn't feel protective; it felt grubby, tawdry. It reeked. Like the inside of Jackson's cast probably had when the doctor sawed it off to reveal his secret festering wound. And what could she possibly be protecting him from, anyway? It was all a lie. Aunt Helen was a lie.

I blinked. Now both her hands rested in her lap. I had imagined it. Or had I? I blinked again and her hands were still resting primly on her own person. She looked at me then, feeling my gaze, and smiled. A true smile. I wondered if I was losing my mind, like Jackson's mother.

When the intermission came, I didn't have to pretend that I felt ill. I asked my dad to drive me home. It was better than running off. Running off prompted questions and I didn't have any answers that I could share with anyone.

My dad fussed a bit but made short work of taking me back to the house. He didn't want to miss any of the laugh riot going on back at the theatre.

It was hot again, or "decidedly warm," as the newspaper kept describing it, but I doubt if I would have slept anyway. I wanted to leave home. Maybe I could dress up as a man and ride west in a boxcar. Me and the grasshoppers.

CHAPTER 16

I walked away from my job the next day. My plan had been to work till the end of July and then take August off to get myself ready for college, whatever that entailed.

But in the late afternoon, when I stood up to visit the ladies' room, Henny called out, " I guess the rich girl deserves more breaks than the rest of us lowly workers."

I quietly snapped. Suddenly I couldn't bear the thought of putting in those last few days. I sat back down and wrote a note to Mary. She was away from her desk at that moment but I taped it to her typewriter. Then I walked out. It was irresponsible, but it gave me a taste of freedom that I didn't remember ever having had before.

When I got to Portage Avenue I crossed over and went into Brathwaite's Drugstore. I browsed at the cosmetics counter, then sat down at the soda fountain and ordered a chocolate sundae. It was the best treat I'd ever had. I dawdled. If I got home too early someone might suspect.

My free feeling didn't last. It was gone by the time I walked down Ferndale Avenue toward home.

The morning after that I went over to Gwen's house early. I dressed for work and left at the same time as usual because I wasn't up to telling Helen and my dad what I had done. They probably wouldn't have cared much, but they would have barraged me with questions.

"I couldn't take it anymore," wouldn't have been good enough for either of them. They would want to know why, and whether I had given proper notice, and if I was going back next summer, and when I had made the decision, on and on and on into next week. So I didn't tell them and I didn't know if I would.

"You quit your job?" Gwen said.

"Yes."

She stood up and started moving around the kitchen. "Do you think they will have hired anybody yet to replace you?" she asked.

"Why? I don't know."

"I need that job, Vi. I need to go downtown and get that job. Will you stay here and watch Warren? It won't be hard; he's not even here, but if he comes home for something to eat or anything. My mum will be out all day, till after I get back, so you don't have to worry about running into her.

"What should I wear?" she called as she ran upstairs.

"Something sensible and white," I said. "They like white in summer and dark colours in winter."

"Can you stay?" she shouted.

"I guess so," I said. There was nothing else on my agenda. It would be a place for me to hang around all day while I was supposed to be at work.

"For sure your mum won't come home and find me here?" I yelled up the stairs.

"For sure," she hollered down. "She's doing a huge house in Armstrong Point. It takes her the whole day."

Gwen came downstairs in an off-white mid-calf skirt and a short-sleeved blouse in the same colour that I'd never seen before.

"How's this?" she asked.

"Good," I said. "Where'd you get the blouse?"

"It's my mum's," she said.

"Won't she kill you?"

"Yes, but I don't care. I need this job. I'm not going to university."

I had figured as much but we hadn't talked about it.

"What about grade twelve?" I asked.

"I don't need it."

"Hmm."

"Why hmm?"

"Just hmm, I don't know."

Everything would be different now that Gwen and I wouldn't be going to school together. I hadn't given it any thought till now.

"Life as we know it is over," I said.

Gwen laughed. "Don't be stupid," she said. She put on lipstick in front of the hall mirror.

"Use a light hand," I said. "They don't hire floozies."

"Do I look like a floozy?" Gwen was panic-stricken.

"No, no. I'm just saying not too much lipstick. They like a wholesome look."

Gwen did look a little like a floozy. She couldn't help it. She was built like her mum with huge breasts and full lips and blonde curly hair. I was sure those lips were wasted on Dirk Botham. I shuddered. His slippery skinny tongue flashed inside my head and I remembered asking Gwen once if he was a nice kisser. I'd wanted to say, "What's it like to kiss a boy with no lips?" but that would have been mean.

Her answer had surprised me.

"I wouldn't know," she'd said primly.

"Are you telling me you've never kissed?" I'd asked.

"I don't want to discuss it," she'd said.

And that had been that.

"Good luck!" I called after her now as she dashed out the front door. "Knock 'em dead."

I felt horrible. I wanted to talk about Dirk and Jackson and Aunt Helen but I couldn't have confided in Gwen even if she had been there. Dirk was her golden boy; she probably thought his tongue was beautiful even if she'd never been allowed to touch it. And the Jackson-Helen thing was too twisted for her; she wouldn't want to hear it. I needed someone else to talk to.

It wasn't too twisted for Mary. She would be able to handle it. But there were other reasons I couldn't discuss it with her. Why had I left work that way? I missed her already. I realized then that I didn't even know where she lived. It was somewhere downtown, on Qu'Appelle Avenue, I thought, but I didn't know the details.

And she didn't have a phone. I'd have to go to Eaton's and wait at the doors for her at quitting time. But I didn't want to run into anyone who knew I had walked out. Maybe I could wear a disguise — a false nose and glasses.

Plugging the kettle in, I prepared to drink some of Gert's instant coffee.

Also, Mary was a blabbermouth. If Gwen got my job, they would sit next to each other and share secrets and the small morsels I had already fed Mary about Jackson would be in Gwen's ears before the end of their first day together. What a mess. How dare she run off and get my job! She hadn't even asked my permission.

I had found out the hard way that Mary was a blabbermouth, that she couldn't keep a secret no matter how hard she tried. There was a boy named Billy Stern who worked on the shipping floor with Lester. I had admired him from afar way back in February when forty below was a good day and I worked only on Saturday mornings. I made the mistake of going into raptures over him to Mary and she passed it on to Lester and he told Billy, who had studiously ignored me ever since. So now I told Mary little about my yearnings, romantic or otherwise, for fear of her talking about them to Perry and the town of Carman and the whole population of Eaton's mail order.

The Jackson and Helen saga would have to wait for Isabelle. And the Dirk stuff too.

Gwen didn't get the job. There were so many people needing work, she said, that the position had already been taken. She had filled out an application form. She cried and I felt bad for begrudging her my position.

Late in the afternoon I went downtown and intercepted Mary as she came out of the mail-order building. I gave her my phone number and Gwen's and asked her to let us know immediately if another position came free.

"I can't believe you just up and walked out," Mary said. "You'll be famous in the mail-order building forever." She laughed.

"Well, like everyone keeps saying, I don't really need the job. And I've got too much other stuff going on right now."

"It must be nice to not have to work," said Mary.

"Not you too," I said. I was tired of people begrudging me my life.

"No, no. I didn't mean anything by it. I was just imagining it, that's all. It really must be nice."

We walked together to Portage Avenue and sat for a few minutes on a bench while I waited for my streetcar.

"I gave Perry the heave-ho," Mary said.

"Good!"

"We fought about having kids and I gave him back his stupid ring. I mean, what's the point in getting married if you don't have kids? Did he really think I could stand to look at only him across the breakfast table for the next fifty years? Lordy, what a muttonhead!"

I laughed. "This is good, Mary. You did right to give him the old heave-ho."

"You never really liked him, did you?"

"To tell you the honest truth, no."

"I realized he's not very good company," said Mary. "He doesn't talk about anything but his work on the farm and I've heard the same stories seventeen times. How many times does a girl need to hear a description of Old Man Fowler losing the lower half of his body under a tractor in a field of wheat?"

"How many times indeed," I said. My thoughts were elsewhere.

"I'm done," said Mary. "I'm not even sure I like him anymore, let alone love him. Maybe I never did. Love him, that is."

My streetcar came and I stood up. I reminded her again to call us if a job came up and stepped on board

"Lester has asked me out," she called after me.

"Swell," I said over my shoulder and found a seat in the shade.

CHAPTER 17

The new cast made a huge difference in what Jackson could accomplish for himself. It ended about two-thirds of the way up his forearm so he could bend his elbow. Aunt Helen gave him some ointment to rub onto the ugly scab in the crook of his arm. I'm sure she applied it herself when I wasn't there but she was self-conscious now if she was nursing him when I was around.

My apology the day of the masturbation episode hadn't been good enough to entirely smooth things over between us. I had been insincere and hadn't succeeded in hiding that. Helen had accepted my apology but had been horribly uncomfortable. I imagined that she wanted to add her own apology to the mix but wasn't able to because of the outlandish circumstances. And there was too much still going on, too many powerful and awkward feelings hanging heavily in the atmosphere of the house. The situation between us seemed unmendable to me; I suspect Helen thought so too.

She knew she was in the doghouse permanently; I could see it in her frightened face. It was a doghouse of her own design and I certainly couldn't get her out of it even if I wanted to. Her arguments on her own behalf died before she could get them out of her mouth. Looking at her face, I watched them die. Hers was a wasted love born in some oddball corner of hell. At least that was the way I saw it. But it was love, nonetheless; when I wasn't busy with plans for her death I felt pity for her. Maybe Jackson reminded her of her lost soldier from Passchendaele.

I despised him, but my body craved him. If I could just kiss him once, I thought, he would want me too. How could he not?

Helen was just an irritant; he couldn't possibly have the same types of feelings for her that I was sure she had for him. I made up reasons why he held himself back from me: my dad, for one. I even convinced myself that he stayed away because he knew if he came close he would be a goner and he didn't want to fall so hard at this stage in his life.

When no one was around I stole a wiener from the fridge, locked myself in the bathroom and practised giving it a hand job. That was what the boys at school called it. My effort was unsatisfactory. My whole hand was too big for the wiener and using just my thumb and first finger had a pernickety feel to it that I knew shouldn't be part of the experience. Isabelle had told me about a girl in grade twelve named Barbara Schulz who put on a glove — one of those white cotton Sunday school gloves — before she touched her boyfriend's dick. She carried it in her purse and then hauled it out when the occasion arose. I don't know how Isabelle knew those kind of details; she knew a lot. I didn't want to be pernickety, like Barbara.

Also, the wiener was fairly limp and it not being attached to anything was a problem. I wondered about fixing it in my dad's vise in the basement. It was attached to his worktable — a present from Helen one long-ago Christmas. When I finally gave up in frustration I decided it was too risky to flush the wiener down the toilet. Imagine if it didn't go down and I had to explain wiener pieces floating. So I took it to the river in a handful of toilet paper. I threw it over the bank and pocketed the toilet paper to take back home to flush. Hopefully some creature would find the wiener and it wouldn't go to waste.

Thoughts of Jackson wouldn't let me be. I could not accept that he didn't want me. Pokes of knowledge nudged me, telling me to wise up, but I couldn't. If he would just allow for it, I could wait forever. Through both our lifetimes I could wait for him.

Benny Boat turned up pretty much on schedule, three days after Jackson had his cast changed, just about the time my dad would have started hinting that it was time for Jackson to hit the road. Benny didn't come back alone. He had a Negro with him that he had met in the sugar beet fields near Taber, Alberta. The Negro's name was Tag and he was even skinnier than Benny. He was the thinnest human being I had ever seen.

They came on a Thursday to hook up with Jackson. They had ridden in on a boxcar and were tired and filthy and starving. Lines ran down their faces where sweat had worked through the grime. And both of them had black rings around their eyes.

"A surefire way of knowing a man's been riding the rails," said Helen. "When the smoke and grit and ash settle in around his eyes."

Tag was so glad to meet Jackson; it was like he was being reunited with a long-lost friend.

"I've heard so much about you, man," he said. "And I like what I heard."

Jackson looked at Benny as Tag shook his hand, and Benny looked away.

I wondered what the heck excellent things Benny'd had to say about Jackson to make Tag warm up to him so immediately. I think my dad wondered too; he looked perplexed. Helen just looked as happy as could be. No one had to explain to her what was so danged great about Jackson.

"Well, I declare," said Aunt Helen, "you're the thinnest man on two feet. I'm surprised the wind hasn't lifted you up and taken you."

"Yes, ma'am," he said.

There was no work for them in the west. As far as the Okanagan, which was as far as Benny went, there were hundreds more men than jobs.

Tag had been even farther, had made it to the coast. He was looking for his younger brother, Duke, who had set out on his own a few weeks earlier to look for work. He hadn't told anyone he was leaving, just left a note for his family to find one morning. Duke was only fifteen and there had been no word of him since his departure. Tag's parents were worried sick and Tag had offered to go searching.

He had started out from Detroit and made the same trek west as Benny, only south of the border. No word of Duke, not a peep, and no work prospects either. When Tag got to Bellingham, Washington he walked over the line into Canada to see if things were any better here. They weren't. But Tag began to hear stories about a young coloured boy from Detroit and he followed those stories to Alberta where he had met Benny.

"Me, too, I had heard of young Duke," said Benny, "but never met him. And someone in Taber said a Negro boy had been through with talk of Winnipeg. He would not stop his talk of Winnipeg, according to the man, so I talk to Tag, convince him, as you say, to return with me. We think his brother could be here."

Aunt Helen insisted on feeding them and washing their clothes. And then the arguments began between her and my dad. Helen thought the men should pitch their tents in the yard and stay for a few days till they were rested and fed to capacity and had some inkling of what they were going to do next.

"What about the offer from Ennis Foote?" she said.

I was still unsure of Helen's motives and I was rooting for her once more.

If our house was a curiosity to neighbours before Tag arrived, it was like a full-blown circus attraction now. There were no coloured people in our neighbourhood. There were very few in the whole of Winnipeg. We didn't have many Chinese or other Asian types either. There was Sam Lee at the laundry on Taché; he was the only one I knew. And there was a Chinese restaurant next door to the laundry, relatives of Sam's, I think, but I didn't know them. My dad wouldn't let us eat Chinese food.

We had Italians in our neighbourhood, Quint Castellano and his extended family, a few Ukrainians and other eastern Europeans like the Popkoviches, and, of course, French and the varying combinations of Métis. But mostly they lived on the other side of St. Mary's Road. In the Norwood Flats we were practically wall-to-wall Anglo-Saxon. No full-blooded Indians and for sure no Negroes.

My dad didn't know what to do. He wanted them out of there.

All Tag talked about was grasshoppers. Coming from downtown Detroit, he had heard of them, of course, and even seen a few in his time, but nothing like what was happening on the prairies.

"I've never been so afraid," he said. "I thought it was the end of the world when I first saw them coming. A plague of locusts."

We were sitting on lawn chairs in the backyard: Tag, Benny, Helen, Jackson, Dad, and me. It was evening of the day they arrived and no decision had been made yet as to where the men would make camp.

"Have you ever been in a grasshopper storm, ma'ams?" Tag looked at Helen and then me. He seemed afraid of my dad. Rightly so.

We both shook our heads, no.

"It's scary, ma'ams, let me tell you. They come in a cloud of millions and black out the sky. I'm not joking. And they leave this juice behind — grasshopper juice — and it makes everything slippery and sticky. You get it on your clothes and on your skin till you want to scream. Man, I've never been so scared. They had to stop the train, didn't they, Ben?"

Benny nodded, yes. Tag was talkative enough for both of them.

"I'm telling you, they stopped the train. It couldn't get any traction because of the slippery glop from the grasshoppers on the tracks."

"Ugh!" I said.

"Yes, ma'am!" he said.

Tag had completed his grade twelve in Detroit that spring. He was eighteen years old. His mum saw to it that he graduated. Tag was the first kid in his extended family to finish high school. There were five brothers and sisters at home (without Duke) and they weren't starving. Both the parents had work. They were furious with Duke and scared stiff for him. So they agreed to let Tag go after him, figuring him to be the sensible one. Tag hadn't been able to find work anyway, so he headed west. There would be one less mouth to feed at home, he reasoned, and perhaps he could find some sort of work and send a few dollars back to his folks along with his brother. He had no doubt that he would find him.

"He's in this city. I just know it," Tag said now.

"You've been a long way from home," said my dad. "What part of Detroit do you live in? I know the city a little."

"Yes, sir. Black Bottom, sir. Brush Street. The only part of the city for the likes of me and my family."

My dad blushed. "Of course, son. I'm sorry."

"No way for you to know, sir."

My dad was quiet after that. He was out of his depth. He didn't know what kinds of questions to ask Negroes.

Helen didn't hang their clothes on the line till after dark when the wind died down. They still wouldn't dry completely clean, but there was no winning against the dust. If anyone could have won the dust battle it would have been Helen; she tried hard enough. She'd be up before dawn to take in the clothes before the wind came up again.

They slept in the yard overnight. Jackson joined them outside. I guess he didn't feel right carrying on in the lap of luxury the way he'd been. No one argued. Tag set up a small umbrella tent of his own, the type with a pole in the centre.

It was good to have Benny back with us. The murmurs of the men lulled me to sleep. Their voices were low and serious: plans for the future, I guessed, what the heck to do next.

I slept soundly that night and halfway through the next morning. It was the best sleep I'd had in weeks, maybe because Jackson was no longer down the hall. I hadn't lain awake trying to get a satisfying breath like I did on so many other nights, when over and over I would breathe in deeply but never deeply enough. I couldn't get that last bit of air inside me, the one I really needed.

It would have been my last day at work. I didn't pretend to go and no one seemed to notice. Whether or not I went to work was so far down on both Dad's and Helen's lists of preoccupations it likely didn't even register. When I looked out my bedroom window I saw an empty yard. The tents were gone. I ran downstairs in my nightie and found Helen in the kitchen.

"Where is everybody?" I asked.

"Gone," she said, busy at the stove.

"What do you mean gone?"

I would never see Jackson again. The worst that could happen had happened. I would never get to kiss him. He would never save me from anything.

"Your father made a grand announcement this morning that they couldn't stay here any longer," said Helen. "He got up on his high horse and told them in so many words that they would have to leave."

"How could he do that?" I asked. "How could he just...do that?"

She turned to face me. "Your dad isn't a mean man, Violet. He's just very...proper. He cares about what people think of him. Like the neighbours."

"The neighbours! The neighbours be damned! Did they have breakfast at least?"

"Yes, of course."

Helen had fed the men oatmeal porridge, fried eggs, toast, and coffee. When they were done eating they'd packed up their tents and clean clothes and headed out. I had slept through the whole thing.

My dad was probably glad of that.

"Where did they go?" I asked. "Did they know where they were going?"

"I'm not sure. They weren't sure."

"Did you tell them about Mr. Foote's offer?"

"I did."

"Where is he?" I asked. "Where's Dad?"

"He's out back with the garage. He bought some paint."

"This is crazy," I said. "So he cares about what people think of him, does he? Does he want them to think that he turns away starving men in their time of need?"

"I'd like to sock him one," Helen said quietly.

She was cooking. And she was cooking for a large group, by the look of it. There was a giant pot of potatoes boiling on the stove and chicken pieces sizzling in the fry pan.

"Are you having a party?" I asked.

"The boys have been invited back for supper," she said matter-of-factly as she stuck a fork into a thigh and flipped it over.

I laughed. "Who invited them?"

"Me."

"Does Dad know?"

"Not yet, no."

"I'll go and tell him," I said and kissed Helen on the cheek.

"Would you mind, dear?" She smiled.

It felt good to be in on something with Helen again.

So the men joined us for supper in the yard. We set the picnic table and they ate like starving wolves. Carrots and stewed tomatoes and corn bread rounded out the chicken and the potato salad and there was rice pudding with raisins for dessert. We drank a gallon of iced tea and laughed a lot.

Jackson seemed glad to be back with Benny. Tag told a few more stories about grasshoppers and even my dad seemed to enjoy himself. I think he felt badly about asking the men to leave and having them back for a meal eased his conscience. He was so torn. I could feel it emanating from him. He felt for them and wanted to help them, but he was also overly conscious of the way it would look to the community, with young me and ever-friendly Helen mixing it up with these strange men. It had been hard enough on him having Jackson in the house without adding a coloured man to the picture.

They had set up their tents in the large field near St. Mary's Road and Cromwell Street. The nearest homes were perhaps two baseball diamonds away. The Willises lived in one of those homes. One of their claims to fame was being one of the poorest families in the Norwood Flats, if not the poorest.

The Willis twins, who had been just fourteen when Sunny disappeared, still lived there with their mum and sister when they weren't in jail. I guess they were having a run of good behaviour if, indeed, it was them that Isabelle and I saw on the dock that night. They would be around twenty-seven now, old bad boys who satisfied their sense of fun by shredding the clothes of young girls out for a night-time swim. But killing clothes wasn't enough to send them back to jail.

Our men had set themselves up on city property and they weren't the only ones there. They had found a spot under the shade of two large oaks. It was a precarious situation. Single men on the move were constantly told to shift, get out of town, even to spend a night behind bars. They were treated like criminals when often their biggest crime was riding a freight car or not informing the relief people that they were leaving home so their mothers could claim their share for her other children.

More often than not there was no crime at all, just the fact of their being on the move instead of staying in one place. The cops could easily charge them with any one of a number of so-called crimes: vagrancy, loitering, trespassing, or being a public nuisance. These men, our men, were transients, not tramps, and I thought I knew them well enough by now, even Tag — he talked so goldarn much — to know that they were good men looking for honest work that for the most part didn't exist for them.

Except for Jackson, of course. I was entirely unsure how good a man he was, and what he was doing living so rough when he didn't have to. But I didn't care.

Dad came into the kitchen for a few minutes after supper when Helen and I were cleaning up.

"I wonder if we could put together some sort of breakfast package for the men," he said.

Helen and I exchanged a glance.

"Sure, Will, we could do that," Helen said. "Go and ask them if they can build a fire over there where they've set up camp."

"Why doesn't he just let them stay in the yard?" I asked after he had gone back outside.

"He just can't, Violet," said Helen. "He just simply can't."

I looked out the window and saw Jackson and Benny out by the lane talking together. They seemed to be arguing. At least Jackson was. Benny was on the receiving end.

My dad sat with Tag at the picnic table. I guessed they were talking about grasshoppers.

Fraser phoned me that evening and we went for a walk by the river.

"Benoit Bateau is back in town," I said.

"Yes," Fraser said, "I heard there were tents set up in your yard."

"Word travels fast," I said.

"Is it true there's a Negro staying at your place?" Fraser asked.

"They're not at our place anymore, and yes, there is a Negro."

"What's he like?" asked Fraser.

"Nice. Kind of funny. He's looking for his younger brother who ran off from home. He's from Detroit and he talks about grasshoppers a lot."

"Yeah. Dirk was saying he was from Detroit."

"Sheesh!" I stopped walking and stared at Fraser. "What's with that dadratted Dirk! What the Sam Hill? Does he spy on people? Does he spy on my family?"

"I think Gwen's mum puts him up to it," Fraser said.

"That's too weird. What does any of this have to do with Gert Walker?"

"She's just a nosy old bat is all. Isn't Gwen supposed to be your best friend? You could ask her about it."

"All her time lately is spent with evil Dirk, master spy and gossip. And clothes killer," I added quietly.

"What?"

"Nothing."

"Did you say clothes killer?" asked Fraser.

"Yes."

"What does that mean?"

"It means that Dirk and the Willis boys sliced my clothes and Isabelle's clothes to bits when we went swimming in the river."

"Jeez."

"Yeah."

"What were you doing swimming in the river?"

"Doesn't what I was doing swimming in the river seem kind of unimportant next to Dirk cutting our clothes to shreds?"

"Yeah, I guess so."

"I should say so!"

"Maybe I could ask him about it when I see him again," Fraser said. "See what he has to say."

"Yeah, that'd be good," I said. "Would you do that?"

"Yes," Fraser said. "I will."

A little swirl of grey dust eddied up in the dry field between us and the motor boat garage. Then I saw a flame and I realized that what I was seeing was smoke; the ground was on fire. Fraser saw it too and we ran to stomp it out. And then we saw another and another. We stomped them out, too.

"Jesus loving Christ," I said. "Our whole world could burn down around us. What if we hadn't been here to put out these fires?"

"Someone else would have," said Fraser.

"Not necessarily," I said. "I think I want to go home now."

I didn't want to see any more fires and be responsible for the safety of the whole neighbourhood.

"My dad's still interested in a new shed," said Fraser as we trudged off over the parched scrub toward my house. "Your aunt phoned him about it."

"Darn it all anyway," I said. "I think I'm going to run away from home."

"Why?"

"Never mind."

"Why?"

"It's…please, never mind." I wasn't ready to share my icky notions about Aunt Helen with Fraser, that was for sure.

"Where are your men staying?" Fraser asked.

"Over in the field behind the Willises' house," I said. "And they're not my men."

Fraser said he would go with me in the morning to seek out Benny. His dad just wanted one man, he said. He didn't want a man with casts on his arms and he didn't have to say which of the other two he didn't want. I wondered if Mr. Foote would dislike Benny because of his French-Canadian accent.

CHAPTER 18

The next morning Fraser and I walked over to the field to find Benny and talk about the shed. The worst that could happen, I imagined, was that we would find the slain bodies of the three men, killed by marauding railroad bulls. The railway police had a bad reputation for violence.

We found them all right. So far no one had murdered them or driven them off. Jackson was playing solitaire with a grubby old deck of cards. Benny and Tag were sitting in the scrub a little ways off from their camp. Benny looked to be in a trance; Tag seemed a little twitchy, like the trance thing wasn't coming easily for him.

"Benny sometimes goes into trances," I explained to Fraser.

"Great," he said. "My dad'll be pleased."

I tossed an almost full pack of Sweet Caporals onto the ground next to Jackson's cards.

"Tailor-mades!" he shouted.

Tag was there in an instant and even Benny wasn't so far gone that he didn't interrupt his efforts.

All of us lit up except for Fraser.

When I introduced him, the three men said hello through clouds of smoke.

"Fraser's dad needs a man to build him a shed," I said.

I wondered if they would think Fraser was feeble because he couldn't build a simple shed for his dad. These hard times were complicated. So often people wouldn't know if their work was of value, like in my dad's case with the garage, or if they were being offered charity in disguise. This case had even more sinister reasons in my eyes, connected to Aunt Helen's middle-aged desperation and her search for one more sunny day.

"They live on Monck Avenue not far from here," I said. "His name is Ennis Foote and he's a pretty grumpy guy, but his wife's nice and his son's okay." I gave Fraser a little shove and he grinned. I wanted Jackson to think that Fraser and I were a couple, that we had sexual intercourse regularly in all kinds of interesting positions and places.

"My dad's not grumpy," Fraser said.

"Yes, he is," said I.

"No, he isn't," said Fraser. "He's just quiet and a little opinionated."

"Just the one man?" asked Benoit.

"I'm afraid so," I said. "It won't be a fun job for you, Benoit, but it will get you a few dollars, a few meals and a place to pitch your tent."

"What about these two?" he asked Fraser. "Can they camp with me in your father's yard?"

"Hmm, I don't know," said Fraser.

I did know, or at least, I was almost positive, but I couldn't bring myself to say it and Fraser didn't say anything more.

Tag knew.

"I'm going to sign up with a relief camp," he announced. "I hear they feed a man pretty well and I should check them out for signs of my brother."

"Those are horrible places, Tag," I said.

"Better than starving," he said as he lit another cigarette. "Or going to jail."

"Maybe." I wasn't so sure.

Single men out of work in those days were considered dangerous. The politicians wanted them gone, out of sight. They feared a revolution from these men with time on their hands. They didn't want them hanging about listening to agitators spouting off about rising up against the system. The agitators were referred to as commies or Bolshies. In reality, most of the men were too tired and hungry to read pamphlets containing words like proletariat and bourgeoisie. But the government couldn't see that.

My information came from listening to my dad and Mr. Larkin talk. Sometimes Aunt Helen, too.

Relief camps had been set up all across the west, where the men were paid as little as twenty cents a day to do back-breaking work, often work that could better be done by a machine — a bulldozer or a steam roller — or work that didn't need doing at all. Tag, who already looked too skinny to survive one more missed meal, would die in a relief camp; I was sure of it.

Jackson's casts would come off in another week or so. Till then, he said, he would bide his time. They would ask the Footes if he could stay in the yard with Benoit.

"If I can't, I can't," he said. "I'll make do."

Fraser nudged me and pointed with his chin to the Willises' backyard past the scrubby elders and wild honeysuckle in the field. The Willis twins stood there staring at us, or at least in our general direction; they were too far away for me to know for sure. Dirk Botham stood with them.

A shiver slid through me like so many tiny snakes. I waved automatically. No one waved back.

I was sure if the Willises realized I was the same small girl who lost her sister all those years ago they would have waved back. But they weren't thinking about babies or their pretty mothers or the way they had helped in the search, lent a hand in 1925. They probably didn't even remember. At least one of them was dim-witted, according to local legend; word was Lump Willis had been deprived of oxygen at birth. That was one of the usual reasons for dim-wittedness.

Anyway, now they were walking swiftly toward us. Dirk was walking backwards in front of them, waving his arms and talking loudly, although I couldn't make out what he was saying. Then all three of them stopped and the Willises concentrated on Dirk's words.

"You wave, Fraser," I said.

He did so the next time they looked our way, but they didn't respond to him either. Not even Dirk. They didn't retrace their steps but neither did they come any closer. I imagined that it was Fraser's presence that stopped them in their tracks. Dirk would have pointed out to them that there was no point in messing with the local cop's son.

The Willises were notorious in our neighbourhood for growing up to be actual criminals. Both of them had graduated from juvenile detention homes to jail as they grew older, for property crimes and worse. One of them beat a fellow inmate so badly that the man lost an eye, or so the rumour went.

What was Dirk doing with these guys? And how could they stand him?

When Fraser and I were plodding back over the field, I said, "Could you tell your dad to keep an eye on those Willis guys?"

"They weren't doing anything, Violet."

"Staring is something. Walking quickly toward us is something."

"Yeah, but they were practically staring from their own backyard. My dad would be more interested in doing something about the guys they were staring at."

"Okay, never mind."

"What the hell was Dirk doing with them?" Fraser said.

"I don't know. It scares me a bit. Maybe you could get your dad to keep an eye on him."

"Dirk Botham's dad is one of the mayor's inner circle," Fraser said. "Practically his right-hand man. My dad doesn't like Dirk, but I can't see him keeping an eye on him, as you say."

"Well, maybe you could just mention to him the sinister activity we just witnessed."

Fraser sighed. "Maybe."

We went back to our house and reported what had gone on to Aunt Helen. Not about the Willis twins and slimy Dirk but about Benoit building the shed.

"I'll stop over this morning, Fraser, and see your mother," Helen said.

If she had anything to do with it, Jackson would be safely ensconced with Benny in the Footes' backyard before the sun set. She didn't say this, but I knew she was thinking it. I sure as heck didn't know what else she was thinking. How far did her imaginings go with Jackson? Did she want to marry him, have his children?

"Did you mention to your dad about the fires we saw by the river last night?" I asked Fraser as he was leaving.

"No."

"Don't you think maybe you should?" I asked.

I could tell I was getting on Fraser's nerves by now, but the whole of life seemed to be getting away on me. I needed outside assistance, maybe from a grouchy policeman who had once made an impossible promise to my dad. Maybe he could help to keep the bewildering world from flattening the good people in it. It was his job, wasn't it?

"My dad can't stop the fires, Violet," Fraser said.

"But maybe he could tell the fire department guys and they could set up patrols or something."

"I think they already do that," said Fraser.

Tears filled my eyes and I turned away but Fraser caught them and put his arms around me right there in the front yard. He led me to the front step and we sat for a while just being quiet. Then he headed off home.

When I went back in the house Helen was on the telephone with Mrs. Foote. Fraser's mother was a religious sort. It wouldn't be hard for Helen to convince her that harbouring Jackson was God's work in one way or another. Maude Foote was almost famous for the breakfasts she offered out her back door, much to Ennis Foote's chagrin. Unlike Helen, though, she was quick to send the travellers on their way. Fraser's dad thought that hunger was a character flaw, like greed or pride. But he didn't stand a chance against the fire that Jesus worked up in Maude Foote's blood. That fire could burn down any objections to getting some food into a hungry man's stomach. Hell, that fire could burn the whole day down.

CHAPTER 19

Things worked out okay for Benny and Jackson for the next week or so. But not for Tag. A couple of days later I stopped by his camp on my way home from Wade's drugstore and there he was, sitting on the ground beside his tent whittling away on a sharp stick. He wasn't alone; Warren and Tippy Walker sat with him. Warren honed his own stick, doing at least as good a job as Tag. Tippy whapped her tail against the ground when she recognized me, raising a low-lying cloud of dust.

"I see you two have found each other," I said.

"Hi, Violet," said Warren. "We were just talking about you and your family."

Tag silenced Warren with a look.

"Nothing bad, I hope," I said, wondering what on earth could have caused that look from Tag.

He changed the subject. "My little buddy here is showing me how to protect myself from a grizzly bear should one happen by."

"I don't think a sharp stick will do it," I said.

He laughed.

I rummaged through my bag of drugstore items and came out with some mixed nuts and a Burnt Almond chocolate bar that I had bought for Tag.

His eyes grew big, especially at the sight of the chocolate bar.

"Violet, are you sure?" he said.

"I'm very sure," I said.

Warren tried not to look at the treats. He knew how much Tag needed them. I reached into my bag again and came out with a small Jersey Milk bar that I had bought for myself and gave that to Warren.

A little stream of drool escaped his mouth when he spoke. "Thanks kindly, Violet," he said.

"Any sign of your brother?" I asked Tag.

He shook his head. "No. No luck there, I'm sad to say."

"How did you make out with the relief camp people?"

"Not so good," he said. "They closed down all the camps last month. There's no such thing anymore."

"It's probably for the best," I said and wiped the sweat off my forehead with the back of my hand.

The day had been hot and clear in the morning, but by lunchtime clouds had pushed in from the west, bringing a dampness with them that made a person want to lie down and rest.

Tag stood up and went into his tent and came out with a small threadbare rug that he folded and set on the ground next to them.

"Sit down, Violet," he said.

I did so, fixing my skirt carefully around my legs.

"Thanks, Tag," I said. "So what now? Will they give you some kind of relief payment while you hunt for Duke?"

"Nah, I don't belong here, they said. They want me gone."

"I'm sorry," I said. "So is that what you're going to do then? Go home to Detroit?"

"I don't rightly know. I don't want to go home without Duke. For the time being I'm going to keep on whittling on this stick till Warren here tells me it's done."

Warren tested the point on his own stick by poking it into his own thigh and saying, "Ouch."

Tag and I laughed.

Warren stood, hitching up his pants. They were way too big for him. "Tag's gonna come and stay at our house," he said. "I'm gonna ask my mum."

Tag and I exchanged a glance.

"Just till Benoit and Jackson are done over at the Footes," said Warren. "And then he can hook up with them again."

It wasn't for me to stomp Warren's idea into the dirt. Gert Walker would do that soon enough. So I just wished them both luck as I got to my feet and continued on my way across the field.

"Watch out for grasshoppers!" Tag shouted after me.

I felt them crunching and dying beneath my shoes. I turned back and waved. It was an effort to raise my arm.

Please go home, Tag, I said out loud to myself. Duke's not here. If he ever was, he's gone now. He's likely home safe with your parents.

"Don't leave without saying goodbye!" I called over my shoulder.

"He's not going anywhere!" Warren hollered back.

By the next morning the scrub field had been deemed off limits by the police, and a few men, including Tag, made a new home for themselves beside the river under the Norwood Bridge.

That afternoon I was over at Gwen's house playing crokinole with her and Dirk and Fraser.

The pressure was on Gwen to get any kind of job now. If she wasn't going to take her grade twelve, she couldn't just be mooning around the house, as Mrs. Walker put it. As though Gwen didn't do every single bit of work in that house, except maybe snap the odd bean.

The four of us sat at the kitchen table. The kitchen was the coolest room in their house when the stove wasn't on. A giant oak shaded a goodly portion of their yard.

We drank Cokes as we played. I had brought them from home. Mrs. Walker didn't believe in Coca-Cola. That was what she said, as though it were its own religion or something. She didn't disbelieve enough not to enjoy a glass when I provided it, though, so I figured it was just that she wasn't willing to spend the money on it but was too proud to say so.

She was at the counter snapping beans.

"What are you doing hanging around with the Willis brothers?" I asked Dirk.

He and Mrs. Walker exchanged a quick look and Gwen stared at me and then at Dirk.

"I haven't been hanging around with them," he said in his flat voice.

"We saw you over in their yard," I said. "Fraser and me. We even waved at you, but you didn't wave back."

I was enjoying myself. Gwen obviously didn't know about Dirk's new best friends.

"The Willis twins have been treated unfairly, if you ask me," said Mrs. Walker. "They're not such bad boys. I swear once or twice when they were sent to jail it was a set-up."

"Why on earth would you think that?" asked Gwen. "Do you know them?"

"I've known their mother forever," said Gert.

"You've never told me this before," said Gwen.

"I was never asked," she said, as if there were any reason in the world that Gwen would have asked her about grubby Mrs. Willis.

Fraser was telling Dirk about how his dad's new shed was turning into a garage. "Benoit talked him into it," he said.

"Who's Benoit?" Dirk asked.

"One of the men who built Vi's dad's garage," said Gwen, "as if you didn't know."

I could see her mother's posture tighten up over her yellow beans.

"Yeah," said Fraser. "My folks went over to Violet's place to have a look at what had been done there and my dad was pretty impressed. I'm helping some. Dad figures I can learn a thing or two from Benoit."

Mrs. Walker snorted. A mean snort, not the kind Gwen made when she laughed.

"About the Willis boys…" I tried to interrupt. Enough about sheds! Fraser should have been helping me out.

"What does your dad need with a garage?" asked Dirk. "That old Studebaker he drives looks like it wouldn't make it to the end of the block."

Fraser laughed. "Yeah, it's an old wreck. But he likes it. And, anyway, he's saving for a new car. When he gets it he'll already have a place to keep it. I think it's a great idea."

"I think so too." I stared at Fraser with what I hoped was a stern look on my face. "My dad's really happy with ours," I said through clenched teeth.

Fraser's face took on a quizzical look and I sighed loudly.

We played without talking for a while, the only sounds the wooden pieces knocking against the sides of the crokinole board and Mrs. Walker snapping her beans.

"Well, I declare," Dirk said quietly.

"What?" said Gwen.

He was looking out the window, past the yard to the field that edged on to the golf course, where we had played baseball in younger cooler times. Warren's field. We followed his gaze: Warren and Tag were throwing a ball back and forth. Tippy was leaping about with them, part of the game.

"Mrs. Walker, come and have a look at this," Dirk said and stood up to make room for her by the window.

"What?" said Gwen again, irritated by now with what I suspect she saw as the unnatural pairing of her mother and her boyfriend against what they saw out the dirt-streaked window.

Mrs. Walker didn't say anything. She just scooted to the back door and shouted, "Warren! Get over here! Get over here right now!"

Warren and Tag stopped their game of catch and looked at her.

"Now, young man!" she shouted again when no one moved.

Warren looked to be speaking a few words to his friend and then he walked toward the house, Tippy at his side with her tail down.

We all continued staring out the window, except Mrs. Walker who waited on the stoop till Warren was at her side.

Tag headed back across the field, to the bridge and his camp there, I supposed.

Dirk was smirking.

"What gives?" said Fraser.

"Gert doesn't like Warren's new friend," I said.

She slapped Warren; we all heard it — it had to be his face. Tippy snarled and Gwen rushed to the door to hold the dog back from attacking her mother.

Sic her, girl; sic her, I said silently.

Gwen tied Tippy to the bottom of the stoop, then followed her mother and brother back into the house.

Warren was crying. "Tag's my friend," he said to his mother. "We share secrets."

"No, he's not your friend and I don't want you going anywhere near that man again." Gert turned to me. "You see, Violet? You see now?"

So it was my fault.

"What gives?" said Fraser again. He must have wanted a better explanation.

"I gotta go is what gives," I said.

"Can you believe he asked me if that filthy vagrant could stay with us?" Mrs. Walker addressed Dirk now.

Fraser came with me. We left through the back door. An angry slap mark hid Warren's freckles. I tousled his rust-coloured hair as I passed him and he looked up at me with a sad, perplexed little face. I looked back at Mrs. Walker.

"He has to learn," she said.

Gwen crouched before him and said, "I'll take you to Happyland later, Pipsqueak. We'll go for a swim."

"We'll all go," I called back.

Gwen followed Fraser and me out and we left Dirk with Mrs. Walker. I hoped Warren would go to his room, away from the two of them.

"Dirk smells like a dentist's office," Gwen said.

Turning to look back, we saw him and Mrs. Walker on the stoop with their heads together as though they were discussing auditions for the school play.

"Look at my mother," Gwen said, walking backwards for a step or two.

Fraser and I clomped along beside her.

"I better go back and see to Warren," she said and ran back home.

We went swimming that evening after supper: Warren and Tippy and Gwen and Fraser and me. Happyland wasn't much of a pool — a simple wooden enclosure fed by the Seine River. But it was big enough to cool off in, deep enough to dive in or drown in, dirty as the dickens.

My friend Isabelle was there and we smoked together. She could roll a cigarette with one hand. She only had enough tobacco for one — she had stolen it from her dad (just like me) — but she shared it, puff for puff.

Fraser and Gwen played with Warren and Tippy while I smoked with Isabelle.

I told her about the cut-up clothes; she already knew. Someone had heard the Willises talking and laughing about it at a coffee shop downtown.

"Do you want to do anything about it?" she asked me.

"Like what?"

"I don't know, some sort of payback."

"No, I don't think so," I said.

I pictured something feeble on our part that would mildly inconvenience them, like burning a poo-filled paper bag on their porch. Then they would follow up by doing something horrendous to us, the crowning glory of the Willises' career in crime, something that would be the worst possible thing that could happen to anyone in the entire history of the universe.

After a good cooling-off, the others came up to us, ready to go.

"See ya, Isabelle," I said, standing.

"See ya, Vi. I'm around if you ever need anything." She winked. "Or if you change your mind about that other business."

"What on earth did she mean by that?" Gwen asked.

We were walking home down back lanes, past plum trees not quite ready for picking.

"I'm not sure." I laughed. "Potato whiskey, most likely. She knows where to get it."

"Good grief," said Gwen.

She had never taken to Isabelle. She couldn't get past her stained tobacco fingers. I liked her fingers and tried to get mine to look like that — like hers and Jackson's — but I couldn't manage it. Sometimes I wanted to be Isabelle, even for just one day.

CHAPTER 20

Several days after our swim I sat with Gwen on her back stoop helping her shell peas. Warren and Tippy were out in the field. We saw them walking slowly towards us, which seemed odd. They usually ran and leapt.

Warren looked scared when he entered the yard.

"What's the matter, Squirt?" asked Gwen.

"I threw up," said Warren, "and my head hurts."

Gwen put him to bed with a bucket beside him on the floor in case he had to throw up again.

"Too much sun," she said.

The next day Warren was fine.

Two days later his right leg ached but he mentioned it to no one at the time.

The day after that, Tippy barked. The quietest dog in the world barked for the first time any of us knew about. Gwen and I were sitting on her stoop talking about what a jackass Dirk was and it took both of us a moment to realize who was causing the ruckus from out in the field. It was Tippy, all right — barking and carrying on — running towards us where we sat and then back towards the middle of the field. Like Rin Tin Tin might have done.

Once we understood her, we ran to follow. We found Warren crawling slowly through the weeds. His eyes were unnaturally bright; he looked like he was watching a horror show at the Baddow Theatre, something way too scary for anyone his age to see, for anyone to see.

A few inches from his outstretched right hand was an old board with four gopher tails nailed neatly to it. Gwen and I carried him to the house and laid him on the chesterfield. I phoned Aunt Helen. Warren's right leg was so weak he hadn't been able to walk. He had crumpled to the ground on his way to the golf club where he was going to sell his tails to the greenskeeper.

He turned to me. "Violet, would you mind going back for my gopher tails? That was a good morning's work."

"For sure, Warren," I said. I headed right out so he would have one less thing to worry about. I found them and put them under the stoop. I fought back my tears; he didn't need to see those.

Aunt Helen was there when I got back.

I told him where I had put the tails.

"Thanks kindly, Violet," Warren said.

"Warren, dear," said Helen, "can you bend your head down to your knees?"

He bent down all right but he bent from the hips with his spine held straight and rigid.

"I feel quite stiff," he said.

"Violet, phone your father and tell him to come over right now with the car. We're going to take this young man to the hospital."

Warren was put in isolation and given a serum that was thought to be effective if administered early on.

Gwen tortured herself. "Why didn't I recognize the symptoms sooner?" she said.

"Why would you?" I said.

"We shouldn't have gone swimming at Happyland," she said.

"I don't know," said I. "Surely it takes longer than a few days to take hold."

By the end of the week Warren couldn't stand up without help. His right leg was almost useless and his left one was weak.

We were all put under quarantine: Gwen and her mum, me, Helen and Dad, all those who had been in contact with him that day. We couldn't leave our houses for three weeks.

Most often polio was connected to swimming places, where other kids splashed and swallowed and spat and peed. But Gert Walker didn't blame Happyland Pool or the Red River or any of the other places where Warren played. She believed that the disease came from the Negro named Tag. She made no secret of this and I prayed to any entity that might be listening that he was safely home on Brush Street in Detroit.

CHAPTER 21

One day ran into the next during our time in quarantine. It was an island of time, separate from the rest of our lives, before or after. A sign was posted on our front door explaining why everyone was to avoid us. I felt like a leper.

But the three of us were lepers together and it wasn't unpleasant. No one could expect anything from us. And I didn't have to worry about Helen and her Jackson-related activities.

I went through my old Hardy Boys books, getting them in some kind of order for Warren. I read *Middlemarch*; my dad read *Ulysses* (it irked him but he forced himself to finish it); Helen sewed. The Safeway delivered groceries and Wades delivered drugstore items. Mrs. Larkin and other neighbourhood women dropped off food and magazines and games and left them on our front steps.

Mr. Larkin brought library books and shouted encouragement to us through the closed front door. "Everything and everyone will be waiting for you when your time is up," he yelled.

We played a new game called Monopoly for hours at a time and cribbage and Parcheesi and Snap. Snap scared my dad out of his wits.

"Please don't shout so loudly," he pleaded to Helen and me. "And I know it has to be sudden, but for heaven's sake!"

He wouldn't play Snap with us more than a few times because we couldn't seem to tone it down.

I talked for long stretches on the phone to Gwen and to Fraser. That also made my dad nervous.

"What if someone is trying to get through to us?" he said.

"Who?" I asked.

"I don't know," he said. "Someone."

Helen wrote letters. She had a lot of people to write to. I wondered how badly she longed for another life — her own life. She could have it now I was grown. Did she not feel that she was wasting away with her brother's family? I tried to talk about it with her but she wasn't very forthcoming. For the first time in my life I saw the sadness in Helen and it was as big as Asia. I asked her about her soldier and all she would tell me was that his name was Joe and he came from Montreal.

That's where my dad and Helen grew up, in a big house on Hutchison Street, close to Jeanne Mance Park. And that's where the two of them went on living after the deaths of first their father and then their mother. Helen was almost through nursing school at the Royal Victoria Hospital at the time but Dad was just a boy of thirteen. The Palmers weren't as well-to-do as my mother's family but there was no shortage of money, so they were able to keep on in the house.

"Why weren't you in the war, Dad?" I asked one evening toward the end of our confinement.

"I wasn't old enough till the last year of the war. And by that time there were too many people interested in keeping me safe. With Major Helen Palmer at the helm." He chuckled.

"You should be grateful you had so many people looking out for you," Helen said, knitting needles clickity-clacking away.

"I was shipped off to Winnipeg when Helen went overseas in 1917. I stayed with your mother's folks till she and I got married the next year. Actually, truth be told, we even stayed on with them for a good while after we were married. They were old friends of my parents, Anne's folks. Your grandpas were at the University of Toronto together."

"You got married when you were eighteen?" I asked. "That's just one year older than I am now!"

"I was very mature for my age." My dad laughed. "And being married was a good reason not to go to war. Everyone was very much for it. It was a darn good thing your mother and I happened to love each other. She was twenty — two years older than me."

"Why didn't you tell me this before?" I wondered aloud.

"I don't know," said my dad. "I guess you never asked." He set his book aside. "There was a lot of talk about conscription by 1917. So a marriage, a place at the university, excellent prospects for my future with a well-known Winnipeg law firm — all those things conspired to keep me safe and in this country. I must say I was swept along."

"Conscription is when they force you to go. Is that right?" I asked.

"Yes."

"Do you ever wish you had gone?" I asked. "To war, I mean."

"Hmm. Sometimes I feel as though I missed out on an experience, a huge one, but I can't argue much with the opportunities I was given for a comfortable future. And I was so fortunate in marrying your mother, and having you."

"And Sunny," I said. "Don't forget Sunny."

"And Sunny." He sighed.

We listened to Helen's knitting needles for a few moments.

"As it turned out," Dad went on, "conscription didn't become law till January of 1918 but no one knew when the war was going to end, of course."

"So you were just nineteen years old when you had me," I said.

"Yup. And your mother was twenty-one. We were just a couple of kids, really, with a lot of help for a while from your mother's family."

On another night we talked about Warren and how bad it could get and what would become of him and how we could help if Gert would let us.

And the three of us imagined the things we would do when we were free.

I pictured adventures with Isabelle and kisses from Jackson and maybe Fraser and then later the same day I would see myself like Thomas Hardy's Jude, when his studies consumed him, before it all fell to pieces. I would be out in time for the beginning of the university year. Maybe an academic life was what I was cut out for. But I had little doubt that at a word from Jackson I would still have run off to the sugar beet fields of Alberta.

My dad wanted to go fishing on the Lake of the Woods.

Helen talked about a trip to the Queen Charlottes but I think it was just for show; her heart wasn't in it. She taught me some of her recipes and she cold waved my hair. One day as she curled a lock of my hair around her finger, I grabbed her hand and held it to my face.

"I'm sorry," I said.

"Whatever for, dear?" said Helen.

I had no answer for her and we went back to the project of my hair. She was very gentle with me after that, more than ever before. But only for a little while. I worried sometimes that Helen would die before I was able to go on without her.

We all three got to the point where we were snapping at each other. And my dad and I slept more than usual. I dozed late into the mornings and he took afternoon naps, something he had never allowed himself before.

And then one day when I woke up, it was over. The quarantine notice was taken from the door and the three of us ventured out into the quiet late-summer world.

CHAPTER 22

The day our quarantine was lifted Gwen and I went to visit Warren. First, I ran his gopher tails over to the golf club so I'd have something good to tell him. He was no longer in isolation and had been moved to the King George Municipal Hospital in Riverview. The number of polio cases was turning into an epidemic. Warren had been one of the earliest victims. He was confined to his bed but his right leg wasn't paralyzed. He could get better.

He was in a room with three other boys, two worse off, one not so bad. The one boy was sitting by Warren's bed and the two of them were finishing up a game of Chinese checkers when we arrived. The boy stood quickly with the help of crutches, the kind that stopped at the elbow and had leather cuffs around the forearms. He offered to give up his chair.

"This is Robert," said Warren. "Robert, this is my sister, Gwen, and Violet, my sister's friend."

"Hi, Robert," I said. "You're pretty good with those crutches."

He was probably wearin' on to twelve years old, as Warren might have put it.

"Yeah, they're okay once you get used to them," he said.

"I'll probably be on crutches soon, myself," said Warren. "And then a cane and then nothing. That's the way it's gonna go."

Not even Robert could look at his bright young eyes. It was too dangerous to talk out loud like that about what was going to happen. What if the devil heard you and decided you needed to be knocked down even further?

"Things are pretty good now that I'm not in isolation anymore," he said. "How's Tippy?"

"She's sad," Gwen said. "She misses you."

"Can you bring her to see me?" he asked.

"I'm pretty sure they don't allow dogs in hospitals," Gwen said.

"Tell her I'm comin' home soon," Warren said. "Don't let her think I'm not comin' home."

"I'll try, Squirt," Gwen said.

When I gave him his eight cents from the gopher tails he told me to give it to his mum. I wouldn't. I'd save it for him till he got out.

"Here's a Hardy Boys book," I said and set a copy of *The Secret of the Old Mill* on his bedside table.

He picked it up and it slipped out of his hand onto the floor.

"Oops," he said. "My fingers are a little weak on the one hand."

I hadn't known that. I picked up the book and placed it next to him on the bed.

"Thanks kindly, Violet," he said, "I really like the Hardy Boys."

"So do I." Robert smiled shyly.

"Warren can lend it to you when he's done," Gwen said.

"You can have it first if you like," said Warren.

"No!" said Robert. "You read it and then I'll read it and then we can talk about it."

"Okay," said Warren.

One of other two boys in the room was lying on his back staring at the ceiling. The other one was on a rocking contraption that moved back and forth; he stared straight ahead as he rocked.

"Where's Mum?" Warren asked.

It was the question Gwen was dreading.

"She sends her love," Gwen said. "She had to go to school today. Classes start on Tuesday."

"So the school's dirty already?" he asked.

"Probably not," said Gwen. "But she was called in for some reason or another."

"No first day of school for me this year," said Warren.

"I guess not," said Gwen. "That's not so bad, is it, Squirt?" She pushed his hair back from his forehead. "Your hair could use a bit of a trim," she said.

"No, that's okay."

Robert had moved away to look out the window.

"Gwen?" said Warren.

"Yes?"

"I was wondering if you could not call me Squirt anymore."

"Sure, I think I could manage that. What would you like to be called instead?"

"Warren would be good."

Gwen and I both laughed.

I couldn't think of anything more to say. I smiled on like a fool and was dangerously close to tears.

"Ernie Pluotte and his mum came to see me this morning," Warren said, "but Mum still hasn't come by. It seems kind of weird to me."

"We'll tell her you're anxious to see her," I said and Gwen gave me a "shut up" look. I should have stayed quiet.

For a while longer we chatted about the things Warren was going to do when he got out. One of them was go to see the Winnipeg Football Club play at the Osborne Stadium.

"There's been some talk about changing their name to the Winnipeg Blue Bombers," I said.

"Really?" said Warren. "That'd be great; what a great name!"

"I think so, too," I said.

"Fritzie Hanson's my favourite player," he said. "He almost single-handedly won the Grey Cup for them last year."

"You're my favourite," I said and kissed Warren on the forehead. I think it surprised us all: me, Gwen, and Warren, anyway. But I couldn't help myself; it just happened. I hoped no one minded too much.

We headed for the door.

"Be extra nice to Tippy," he said.

From the hallway I heard Robert say, "You're really good at talking to grown-ups."

Warren chuckled. "They're not really grown-ups," he said. "They were kids not that long ago, even though they've always been older than me."

We walked to Osborne Street to catch a streetcar.

"So what's with your mum?" I asked.

"She doesn't want to come to the hospital."

"Why not?"

"Because she's an evil witch dressed up like a regular person."

I stared at Gwen.

"Let's not talk about her," she said. "I hate her."

I put my arm through Gwen's for the rest of the walk to the streetcar stop.

A warm shifting breeze worried the leaves on some trees and not on others, on one branch of a shrub and not on others. It stirred the hem of Gwen's skirt and not mine.

"I hate wind," said Gwen.

"Gosh," I said. "I hate it too, but this doesn't even qualify, Gwenny. This is barely a breeze."

"I hate it," she said.

On the way home on the streetcar I planned all the vile things I was going to say to Mrs. Walker next time I saw her, which I hoped was never.

"He's just a little boy!" I blurted out.

Gwen concentrated on the passing scenery and I tried for a while to keep my thoughts to myself.

Where did Warren get his optimism, I wondered, with a mum like Gert to learn from? I wanted to bottle him and sell him to the world; no, I wanted to wrap him up safe and take him home and keep him for myself.

Gwen's mum was still out when we got to their place. If only I could booby-trap her house in some way so that she would die. Perhaps an invisible wire at the top of the basement stairs would do it. She could tumble down and land upright on a broom. It could go in at the bottom of her and come out the top. A grisly, impossible death. But I'd have to make sure the trap didn't backfire and kill Gwen.

I didn't want to leave her yet so I offered to make some coffee. We sat with our cups at the kitchen table.

"She doesn't want to go and see him," said Gwen, "so she's pretending she doesn't have time."

"Why?"

"Because she a wicked hag of a woman."

"What else?"

"She thinks polio is a disgrace. She thinks only the children of immigrants and poor housekeepers get it."

"That's just not true," I said. "The opposite of poor housekeepers get it." I explained Helen's theory about all of us being a little too clean.

"My mum would never fall for that," Gwen said.

"But...but...Warren..."

"I know."

"What's going to happen? He's going to need help."

"Violet, I know all this. It's all I think about." Gwen started to cry.

"Oh, Gwen, I'm so sorry. I'll help! I'll help in any way I can."

"I don't know what we're going to do. My mum won't discuss it. She's written a letter to Franklin Roosevelt. Apparently he's got polio and he has some sort of facility down south where people go to get better."

"She wrote to the president of the United States?"

"Yeah. Bright idea, eh?"

"I don't know if she'll get very far with that." I looked out the window past the empty backyard to the scrub field with the golf course beyond. "Where's Tippy?" I asked.

Gwen didn't answer for a moment.

"Gert's had her put down," I said.

"No," Gwen said. "But she's gone. Tip's run away."

"Oh no."

Tippy being gone was probably the second-worst thing that could happen to Warren. At least Gert hadn't killed her. I'd find her.

We mumbled goodbyes when I left Gwen at her place. And we hugged, which wasn't like us.

The phone rang as I walked in the door at home.

It was Mary at her desk at Eaton's telling me to tell Gwen to get right down there. It turned out that a number of the girls hired that summer had been lying about staying on in the fall. Just like me. They were college girls, also like me, and were heading back to school.

"Even some of the ones that were mean to you," Mary said.

She was sure if Gwen turned up quickly she would be hired on.

"Tell her to tone down those breasts of hers," she said, "and wear something dark."

I phoned Gwen immediately and gave her the news. "Mary said to tone down those breasts of yours," I added, "and wear something dark."

CHAPTER 23

Benny and Jackson were still in the neighbourhood. There was a house going up on Crawford Avenue and Ennis Foote put in a good word for Benny. His garage had turned into a thing of beauty, far more resplendent than ours. Mr. Foote had gotten carried away.

Jackson's casts were off by now and he was hired on too, but his arms were still weak. Their tent was pitched in the backyard of the new house along with that of another man who had been hired to help the official builders.

Aunt Helen had this information for me when I got home from Gwen's house. It seemed her first order of business when we were allowed out was to go over to the Footes' place to see what was going on with the men. Mrs. Foote was worried about Jackson hurting himself again. It was rough work for arms so recently broken.

"Did you see Fraser?" I asked.

"No. He wasn't home," Helen said. "I'm sure you'll hear from him later once he hears you're out and around."

Like I needed some sort of reassurance from her. Shut up, Helen, I said to myself. I realized she had been mooning over Jackson these last weeks, probably more than I had, and I wanted to slap her.

"Tippy Walker ran away," I said. "Keep an eye out, would you, and tell everyone you see? We've got to find that dog before Warren comes home."

"How was Warren?" Helen asked.

"He's weak all over and the one leg may be paralyzed. But he's keeping his head up. That's for sure."

"That dear, dear boy."

"Yeah."

"I'll watch out for Tippy," she said.

Helen and Maude Foote had drawn up a plan to take turns providing food for the workers on Crawford Avenue, those with no homes to go to. Helen and I went that evening with a basket of turkey sandwiches and white cake with butterscotch icing. We waited to make sure that the men with homes had gone. Jackson wasn't there.

I guess Helen and Maude got their wires crossed, because Maude turned up too. There was some nervous laughter and it was decided that her egg salad sandwiches could be breakfast. And her banana cake a midmorning snack.

There was a banged-up old cooler in the yard. It sat next to a huge bucket of tar. There was no lid on the tar and it made me nervous to look at it. What if it spilled out onto the clean dirt? What if a bird landed in it? What if a kid thought it was something to plunge his hands into?

"This is Fuzzy," Benny said, introducing the other hired man. "Fuzzy Eakins."

The man had a sleek head of hair and a smooth hairless chest inside his unbuttoned shirt so I don't know where his name came from. I didn't ask.

He grunted a response.

"He is from Vegreville," said Benny, as if that would explain Fuzzy's rudeness.

"Where's Jackson?" asked Helen and Maude together. I knew I could leave it to them.

The two men exchanged a glance.

"Gone for a walk," Benny said. "The boss warned him today, accused him of not, how did he say? pulling his weight."

"He ain't," said Fuzzy Eakins. "He ain't pulled no weight at all. An' he gets equal wages for standin' aroun' takin' up space. I got friends need jobs an' Jack's just blowin' it out."

"Jackson worries about his arms," explained Benny. "He is very careful. Over careful."

"What will he do?" Helen asked.

Benny shrugged. "He talks about going home. But it is not time for him to go."

"What do you mean?" I asked.

"I got friends who could be doin' twice the job that Jack's doin'," Fuzzy insisted.

"Do not call him Jack. He does not like it." Benny was testing the blade on his pocket knife.

"He's a girly," said Fuzzy.

"Tell Jackson to come and see us," Helen said to Benny, "before he leaves, if he does."

"What do you mean it's not time for him to go home?" I asked again.

"He has, how do you say? unfinished business," said Benny.

"What kind of unfinished business?" I asked.

"It is not for me to say."

"Goldarnit, Benoit," I said. "What about Tag? Does anyone know if he found his brother or if he went home, or what?"

"I do not know, said Benny. "He had not found Duke when I saw him a few days ago. I hope he is gone home because if he is not, I do not know where he could be."

"Is that the nigra?" asked Fuzzy.

No one paid him any mind.

"Is that the nigra fella?" Fuzzy repeated, louder this time.

"Shut up, Fuzzy," said Benny. "Go to the icehouse and get ice for the cooler. Be useful, why not."

"What's the...?"

"Go!" Benny said.

Fuzzy shuffled off down the lane.

"I worry about Tag," said Benny. "If he was leaving, he would come to say goodbye. He knows we are here."

Maude began to bustle about, ready to leave.

"How is Warren?" Benny asked.

"He could be worse," I said. "It hasn't affected his breathing or his swallowing, so he's lucky in that way. His one leg's pretty bad. No one knows yet if that will be forever or what all."

"Poor little shaver," Benny said.

"Yeah."

I told him about Tippy, and then Maude and Helen and I headed off down the lane in the opposite direction from Fuzzy. We all agreed we'd rather not see him again.

"If Jackson goes back to Montreal I'd like to at least give him a train ticket," Helen said after we left Maude at her corner.

Jackson wasn't something I could talk about with Helen, so I said nothing.

"His arms will be weak for some time yet," she said. "Say something, Violet."

"Yes, they will," was the best I could do.

I couldn't get a deep breath on the way home. Sometimes I got to worrying that even the shallow breaths I could manage might get more difficult and then where would I be? I might as well have polio — the worst kind.

"Goodness, Violet, you silly goose," Helen said, as we marched home in the falling dusk. "Breathe normally, can't you?"

I shook my head, gasping, "I can't."

She held my hand the rest of the way home and I was able to take in enough air to keep me alive for the time being.

CHAPTER 24

That night I got drunk for the first time in my life. It was a planned occurrence. I put money in one pocket and a pack of cigarettes in the other.

"I'm going to see Isabelle," I announced to Helen and Dad, who were sitting on the verandah in the warm night air. Helen was sewing but it was almost too dark.

"Well, be careful over there," Dad said. "You don't have to do everything and go everywhere on your first day out."

"I don't blame you for wanting to be out, dear," said Helen. "It's been a long three weeks cooped up in the house."

"Don't bring any biting insects home with you," said my dad. "Why can't you visit someone on this side of St. Mary's Road?"

"Because I want to visit Isabelle and I hardly ever see her. Besides, you like her. You said she had gumption."

"That was before I knew she lived in the Taché Block and was going to pass her bedbugs along to you."

"Never mind him," said Helen. "Go out and enjoy yourself. Here, take one of my hatpins with you."

"What for?"

"In case you have to give someone a poke." She tried to hand it to me in its little case but I wouldn't take it.

"I'm not going to be giving anyone a poke," I said. "Can I stay out a little later than usual?"

"No," said Dad.

"Yes," said Helen. "If you take this hatpin with you."

I sighed and put it in my pocket next to my Player's cigarettes.
I was trying out different brands. These ones were pretty good.

"And don't forget to breathe," added Helen.

"Be sure Constable Switzer doesn't catch you up to no good,"
called my dad as I let the screen door go. "And don't be afraid to
call on him if you need' him for any reason."

"Yeah, Dad," I shouted back.

Constable Switzer was a uniformed cop who was on foot patrol
in our neighbourhood at night. He was overweight and wore very
thick glasses. It was hard to imagine him coming to the rescue if
real danger approached. He was friendly enough: he always answered
when we said, "Hello, Constable Switzer." Sometimes he said things
like, "Isn't it a little late for you kids to be out on the streets?" and
we said things like, "No."

I ran over to Isabelle's. Her family didn't have a telephone so I
just had to hope that she would be home. She was. I hadn't been to
her place before but I knew where it was — on the corner of Taché
and Eugenie.

It didn't look so bad from the outside — just a big square brick
block of a building. But it reeked on the inside. I found her last
name, Syrenne, on a mailbox, number 22. The hallways were dim
and I tripped on the stairway up to the second floor before I saw
the broken step. My hand caught me and scudded along the wooden
floor till I had a few goodly slivers.

On my way down the hall I passed a bathroom that was one
source of the overriding stench. It mingled with traces of cooked
cabbage and dirty laundry. I wondered how bubble and squeak
would taste to me the next time Helen served it up.

I knocked on the door of number 22. Isabelle answered.

"Well, Christ on a stick, Violet! Come in!"

She opened the door wide and I entered a tidy little apartment
that smelled of cigarette smoke and lemon furniture polish. It was
so clean I felt as though I should take off my shoes like I'd read that
the Japanese do.

Isabelle had a younger brother, Charles, whom I'd seen around
school. He was fifteen or so. And there were two younger sisters,

Evangeline and Paulette. They were all there and she introduced me around. There was no sign of a mother or father but I knew she had both.

The tiny apartment was dwarfed by a huge oaken dining table. It must have been in the family for years, come with them from Quebec or from France even, who knew.

There was a lump of bedding on the table. I had interrupted Isabelle as she prepared a sleeping place for her two sisters and herself on the table.

"It's just temporary," she explained as she smoothed out the sheets and carefully placed the pillows. "Till the fumigators come to do the bedbugs again."

I guess my dad knew what he was talking about.

Evangeline and Paulette stood in their nighties, watching their big sister fix up their sleeping area. Vangie, as Isabelle called her, held the raggediest old stuffed bear I had ever seen. I wanted to race out and get her a new one. Not that she'd love it more — I knew how teddy bears worked. But I worried that some of the bugs had attached themselves to the bear and that the little girl would be no better off than on her infested mattress.

"Charles, you'll be home till maman gets in." Isabelle was definitely the boss of this family when the parents weren't home.

"Oui," he said.

Isabelle kissed her two sisters and spoke to them in French.

When she closed the door behind us I mentioned my concerns about the stuffed animal.

"She won't give it up," Isabelle said. "My mum takes it to work with her once a week and does a real job on it. She works at a laundry. Just a sec," she said then and stopped off at the bathroom in the hall.

It wasn't till then that I realized Isabelle's family had to leave their apartment to use the bathroom. And they shared it with who knows how many other families. If tiny Evangeline had to pee in the middle of the night she had to leave home to do it.

"What's up, Violet?" said Isabelle once we were on the street.

"I want to get drunk," I said.

Isabelle laughed. "Okay, let's. Have you got any money?"

I showed her what I had. There was a government liquor store on Marion Street just down the block. I'd heard it was easy, for a price, to find an older guy to go in and get you something, but it was closed at that hour so we had to look further afield.

A man named Howard Strachan lived in one of the apartments at the Norwood Terraces a couple of buildings up from the liquor store. He sold stuff to anyone, but there wasn't much of a selection, Isabelle warned. We knocked on his door and he answered in a greying undershirt with suspenders holding up pants that would have fallen down otherwise. His nose was big and pockmarked and red and his grin was ear to ear: he had the look of a clown.

"Hi, Howard," said Isabelle. "Whatcha got?"

"Not much, little lady. Who's yer friend?"

"This is Violet," she said.

"Hello," said I.

"Come in."

The stench of the place was worse than in Isabelle's building. It wafted out and enveloped us.

"We'll wait here, thanks, Howard," said Isabelle, thank the Lord, and he went inside and came back with a pint of clear liquid in a bottle.

"Potato whiskey," he said. "You won't be disappointed. But be careful. Get something to mix with it and be generous with the mix."

"How much?" I asked.

"A dollar should do it," Howard said and I forked over the bill.

We skipped away with our prize, along the wooden sidewalk of Marion Street to Andrews Candy Shop. There we came away with a jug of lemonade and two large paper cups. Isabelle had hidden the bottle in the waistband of her trousers when we were at Andrews. Not everyone was as understanding as Howard about young girls drinking raw potato whiskey. Andrews Candy Shop had a motto: *Our aim is quality and service — a trial will tell.* I was quite sure the lemonade would pass muster.

So we were set. Now, where to go to drink it? I suggested the riverbank by the icehouse, but Isabelle thought that was a boring location. She suggested a vacant lot on Marion so at least we could watch people go by. I was uncomfortable with such a public place so we settled on the steps of Norwood Collegiate on Kenny Street, off the main drag but not as secluded as the river bank.

The first sip of potato whiskey, even mixed with the lemonade, was like a slash of white lightning travelling the length of me.

Isabelle saw to it that I took it easy. She knew what the stuff could do. I brought out my Player's and we smoked like fiends — chain-smoked, lighting them one after the other.

I talked about Jackson Shirt, about how I'd fallen for him and how my Aunt Helen had held his dick in her hands, probably more than once. I sensed that nothing could astonish Isabelle and I was right. Nothing I could tell her, anyway. She took it all in, laughed uproariously in spots and crinkled up her forehead with concern in others, like when I described Gert Walker. I told her about Tag and Duke and how we all hoped they were gone now and about little Warren Walker having polio and his dog having run off.

"The kid you were with that night at Happyland," she said.

"Yeah, him."

"That's awful," she said.

"Yeah," I said. "It's the worst."

I told her about Fraser Foote, about how much I liked him and how much less I wanted to kiss him than Jackson.

"Yeah, it's Jackson I wanna kiss," I said. I was drunk by now.

"It's Jackson I wanna fuck." I had never said that word before, except alone in my bedroom where I sometimes whispered it, and I liked the sound of it coming out of my mouth. "Fuck," I said again. "I'd like to fuck him and have him fuck me."

Isabelle laughed. "Yeah. He is pretty handsome," she said.

"Have you ever been fucked, Isabelle?" I asked.

"Violet, I think you've had enough. I'm going to walk you home. It might take us a while."

"You're a kind person," I said. "I really like you."

"Come on now. Stand up," she said. "I like you, too."

"I love you," I said, as I got to my feet. I was a little wobbly but I soon found my legs.

Isabelle chuckled by my side and we strolled amiably through the night streets.

"I've heard of that guy, Tag, you were talking about," she said.

"You have?"

"Yeah. And I think he's still around. I heard someone talking about him downtown."

"What?" I asked. "Who?"

"Let me check my facts. I might be all wet."

She walked me home, the entire way.

"Do you have a little sister?" she asked at my door.

If she had requested a kiss I wouldn't have been more surprised.

"I did have," I said. "I don't anymore. Someone stole her a long time ago. Why? What makes you ask that?"

"It might be that I heard somebody talking about it. The same guys that were talking about your friend Tag. Actually, it was Dirk Botham and those Willis creeps — the guys that wrecked our clothes."

Nausea took me over and I heaved up potato whiskey and my long-ago supper into the mock orange shrub in front of the verandah.

Isabelle stayed with me till I was done. "I still think we should get them for that," she said, "even though it was my least favourite pair of shorts that they mangled. They used to belong to Charles."

I shivered in the warm night air and sweat ran down my face. I worried that my dad or Helen would wake up and witness the mess I was in. When I was pretty sure I was done throwing up, I sat down beside Isabelle on the steps.

"My sister's name was Sunny," I said.

Isabelle brought her face to within a few inches of mine and said, "Are you okay?"

"I think so. Just kind of shaky."

Her talk about Sunny had sliced through my drunkenness but only enough that I made myself remember to pursue it with her at a later date. Tomorrow.

It was probably just that Dirk mentioned the kidnapping to the Willises in passing, as a point of interest for criminals. He, of course, would know all about it. And the Willises would have remembered that time long ago when they had searched for Sunny in the hope of winning the reward. Maybe they regretted cutting my clothes to shreds if they knew I was the big sister of the kidnapped baby. No. No chance. Their eyes had been only on the money.

I was confused, as usual. Drunkenness certainly didn't help my reasoning powers. I felt dull-witted and ineffective, like a puddle person. Isabelle seemed so clever and decisive next to me. I needed to lie down.

"This Sunny business…" I said.

"Let me put my ear to the ground," said Isabelle, "and see what I can come up with."

I laughed. Her words reminded me of a line from a hymn we used to sing in Sunday school, a thousand years ago. It went: *And they shall bite the ground.*

My friends and I used to practically implode with suppressed laughter at that line. When one of us thought to ask an adult about it, we found that it had something to do with the defeat and death of soldiers. We had pictured people literally biting the ground and it had struck us as hilarious.

I didn't have the energy to explain this stupid story to Isabelle.

"Are you going to be able to get in all right?" she asked.

"Isabelle?"

"Yeah?"

"Don't you find it kind of scary that they knifed our clothes to bits?"

"Yeah, maybe."

She waited till the door closed behind me before she started off down the street.

I'd forgotten to ask her what she believed about the pope, but I think I already knew the answer.

"Fuckin' pope," I whispered and laughed quietly.

Dad and Aunt Helen were in bed. They both called out to me as I made my way to the bathroom and then my bedroom, crashing into more than one piece of furniture along the way.

"Goodnight, all," I said, hoping I didn't sound as odd as I felt.

Fully clothed, I lay down on my bed. The room seemed to whirl around me. I had to keep my eyes wide open to ward off the sick feeling. Sunny. What could Isabelle possibly have heard about Sunny? She would tell me. She was my good friend. Better than Gwen. I started to cry. What if Jackson was fired from his new job and gone before I saw him again? I blew my nose and before long I fell asleep for a short time.

When I woke up my alarm clock said quarter to three. Dad was snoring. I still felt slightly drunk but no longer sick like I had before dropping off to sleep. I crept down the stairs and out the front door. If Helen heard me, tough. She wasn't quick enough to stop me.

CHAPTER 25

Inside the moonswept landscape I wove a clumsy trail to the construction site on Crawford Avenue. I breathed deeply over and over again. It amazed me that the breaths went so far inside me and came so smoothly. Why couldn't I breathe with this kind of ease all the time?

I stood in the back lane and stared at the cluttered yard. The men had built a small fire between the tents and embers still glowed against the dark earth. Then I saw the end of a burning cigarette and made out a form near the dying fire. I could smell the smoke from the cigarette and I knew it was Jackson. He sat cross-legged on the dry dirt.

"Psst!" I said.

He didn't answer.

"Psst!" I said again.

"Who's there?" said Jackson.

"It's me, Violet," I said. It sounded like: *iths me.* I hoped he hadn't noticed. Certain things about being drunk were difficult.

"Violet?"

"Yes. It's me." *Yesh, iths.*

"What are you doing out there? Come here."

"No. You come here."

"You come here."

I went in through the gate and knelt on the dirt beside him.

"What are you doing?" he asked again.

"I wanna kiss you," I said. *Kith.*

"You've been drinking," he said.

"So?"

"You're drunk."

"So?"

"You shouldn't drink."

"Why not?"

"Because."

"Why because?"

"It's unbecoming."

I laughed. "Heaven forbid." Words sounded funny to me. Like, heaven forbid. Had I really said that? Was it something I said on a regular basis?

"Kith me, Jackson," I forced myself to say it. That whiskey was really something.

"No."

"Why? Do you think I'm ugly?"

He chuckled, barely. "No. I don't think you're ugly. I think you're crazy."

"I'm not crazy."

It seemed impossible to me that he didn't want to kiss me. How couldn't he? Isn't that what boys usually wanted to do? Kiss and then fuck?

"Do you hate me?" I asked.

"Would that give you some satisfaction, if I told you I hated you?"

"I don't know. Maybe." It would be better than nothing.

"No, Violet, I don't hate you."

"I don't believe you," I said. "What is it that you hate about me? Is it my face?"

He chuckled again. "You've got a nice face," he said. "I could never hate your face."

"Is it because of Aunt Helen?" I asked.

"Go home, Violet."

"Is it because of Helen?" I asked again. "Are you in love with my Aunt Helen?"

He laughed out loud now. "Don't be ridiculous, Violet. Your Aunt Helen is…well… she's your Aunt Helen. What about Fraser?"

he went on. "Isn't he your boyfriend? I don't want to ruin anything for you."

"You've ruined my whole life if you won't kiss me."

I had no pride. The drink had taken it away.

"This is so unlike you, Violet."

"Unlike me? What do you mean? What am I like?" It angered me that he claimed to know me at all. What did he know? What did I even know?

He did know how badly I hungered for that kiss. He was on his knees now too and he brought his face close to mine.

"Violet," he whispered.

"Jackson," I whispered back.

"Violet," he said again, softer yet. He was so close. He brushed his lips against the corner of my mouth, softly, like a moth. It was barely a tickle, but a rush of sickening desire tore through me. And then he pulled away and stood up.

"I hate you," I said.

That almost kiss wasn't leading to something else and it wasn't because he thought better of it for any good person's reason or even because I tasted like vomit. He did it to torture me; I was sure of it.

"I hate you," I said again as I scrambled to my feet.

"Violet," he said as I tripped through the yard.

That word meant nothing to me.

Aunt Helen's hatpin was still in my pocket and when I felt it there I wanted to drive it hard into my own body.

I didn't look back; I needed every ounce of my remaining wits to get out of there without breaking an ankle in the rubble. With any luck at all, neither Fuzzy Eakins nor Benny Boat had witnessed any part of the fiasco.

My head hurt when I woke up in my bed later on that morning. I thought about Jackson and my stomach rebelled. Then I thought about Isabelle and was relieved to realize there was nothing about my time with her that I regretted. She wouldn't judge me, and she knew far stranger lives than mine. It was okay that I'd confided in her. Had I dreamed the part about Sunny? No.

Later that day with a heavy achy head I walked by Crawford Avenue and saw Benny and Fuzzy at work — no sign of Jackson. I wasn't sure what I was doing there. My plan had been to find Isabelle.

I didn't want Jackson to see my face again so soon. I approached the back fence cautiously. Next time I saw him I planned to be very quiet, maybe not utter a sound. Anything and everything was ruined between us and I would be silent.

Benny saw me and came over. "Jackson was let go this morning," he said.

"Let go?"

"Yeah, sent packing," Fuzzy said as he joined us at the fence. "For not pullin' his weight."

"Go back to work, Fuzz," said Benny.

"You go back to work," said Fuzzy.

Benny sighed and gave his co-worker a look that sent him sloping back to his job, which looked to be removing rusty old nails from lengths of well-used lumber. Benny did have a way about him. Maybe it was all those trances he went into. They gave him a certain power. He had become the unspoken foreman of the job site. But he didn't have enough power to save Jackson's job.

"Where did he go?" I asked.

"I do not know. He said he would look for Tag."

"Does he know that Tag is still around?" I asked.

"No, I do not think he knows anything like that," Benoit said.

"I think he is," I said. "Still around, that is."

Isabelle's words from last night came back to me in partial form.

"How do you know?" asked Benoit.

"I don't know. Maybe I don't know."

Benoit kicked at the dry dirt under his feet. "Jackson left his knapsack here so he will be back for sure before he leaves town."

"Good riddance!" Fuzzy called over.

"Shut up, Fuzzy," said Benoit.

He stared at me then for a long moment. "And… I know there is something else he is here to do that he has not done yet."

"What? What the heck is it you keep hinting at?"

"I cannot say."

"You can't or you won't?"
"It is not for me to say."
"Come on, Benoit."
"No."
"Please tell me."
"No."
"I won't tell that you told."
"No, Violet. Sorry."

I went looking for Isabelle, but I couldn't find her, so I went home and straight to bed. I think Dad and Helen knew that I'd been drinking the night before. They must have heard me throwing up into the bushes; both their windows would have been wide open. But they kindly didn't mention it. They must have discussed it and figured it was best left alone. I was suffering enough without them adding their two cents' worth. Tomorrow I would do something nice for them, I thought. I was asleep before I figured out what it would be.

The next day, the Sunday of the Labour Day weekend, I went back to Isabelle's place. Her brother, Charles, was the only one home. The rest of the family had gone to Grand Beach for a couple of days to stay with an aunt who had a cabin there. A last hurrah before the two little ones were due to start school.

I asked Charles to tell Isabelle that I was looking for her. Then I went home and baked a lemon pie, my dad's favourite.

CHAPTER 26

On Monday, Labour Day, I went to see Benny again. It was the day before university began. Jackson still hadn't been back for his gear.

"I have a very bad feeling," Benny said.

"A regular bad feeling or a trance-like bad feeling?" I asked.

"Regular," said Benny. "Trances, as you call them, do not make bad feelings."

I still didn't have much of an understanding of his hypnotic-type experiences.

"Sorry, Benoit," I said. "What do you call them?"

"I do not call them anything. They need no name."

"Please don't be mad at me right now," I said. "I have a very bad feeling too."

"Something has happened to him," Benoit said. "He should have returned."

"He's dead," I said, and my eyes grew warm.

"No, he is not dead," said Benny, "but something keeps him from returning for his things."

"What'll we do?" I asked.

"Nothing, I am thinking," he said. "I have searched in the evenings, asked men I saw. I went to the hobo camp in Transcona. No one knows him. I think he is gone and without his things."

"What makes you think he's not dead?" I asked.

Benny shrugged.

Back at the house I told Helen about Jackson. She already knew.

"Why didn't you tell me?" I asked.

"I wasn't sure there was anything to tell," she said. "I thought he might turn up overnight."

There were lines and sags on her face that I'd never seen before. I swear they just arrived that weekend, with the news of Jackson's disappearance.

The next day I went to Wesley College to pick my courses. My heart wasn't in it. I chose English, history, French, philosophy, and sociology. I didn't care. I still had no idea what I wanted to be. Physical therapy had seemed like a good idea to me for a day or two after I'd visited Warren. I'd be able to help people like him. But I was pretty sure you needed sciences for that, and sciences and I didn't get along.

When I got home, Helen was waiting for me.

"Let's go over and rummage through his knapsack," she said.

"Isn't that kind of invasive?" I asked.

"No. Not at this point," she said. "What if there's something in there that gives us a clue to where he's gone?"

"Only if Benny says it's okay," I said.

"Benny?" she said. "Since when did Benoit become Benny?"

"Since forever, in my head," I said.

Helen smiled at me from inside her new old face.

"We do not see him for three days," Benny said when we got there after supper. He held up three fingers.

"What do you think of the idea of looking inside his knapsack?" I said.

"I do not think…" said Benny.

"We have to," Helen said. "Get it, Violet."

I went inside the tent and picked it up carefully, noting its exact position against the wall in case Jackson turned up expecting to find things as he had left them. I didn't want to be caught twice, even though we had a dang good reason this time. And this time Helen could be blamed. Holding it to my face, I breathed deeply. When I turned around Benny was at the door of the tent. He saw me do it. I felt the colour rush to the roots of my hair.

He must have known how I felt. He had to be used to women falling for Jackson by now. Look at Helen, and even Maude Foote, for goodness' sake! It had been written all over her egg salad sandwiches. Probably girls all the way from Montreal to Winnipeg had looked at Jackson with that same naked humiliating craving that I had been feeling all summer.

When I took the knapsack outside I looked inside it and saw that the contents were a jumbly mess.

"Hmm," said Benoit. "I do not like this."

"Where's Fuzzy?" I asked.

"He hitchhiked to Grand Beach for today," said Benoit.

"Good," said Helen. "We certainly don't need him poking his nose in."

Benoit dragged over a wooden worktable and I emptied out the contents onto its rough surface. The picture of Bertram Shirt drifted to the ground. Benny picked it up and stood quietly looking at it while I spread out the rest of Jackson's stuff.

"That's Jackson's little brother," I said, in case he didn't know.

Benny was struggling with something; he looked positively ill.

"What is it, Benoit?" asked Helen. "Are you all right?"

"Please," he said. "Sit down. I must tell something to you both."

Helen and I sat down right on the dry dirt of someone's future backyard and Benny sat with us.

"One," Benny said, "I believe Jackson told you he comes from Westmount in Montreal.

"Yes," said Helen. "He told us."

"That world has this year fallen apart. Jackson's father has died and his maman has become…an insane woman."

"Yes," Helen said again, "He told us that too, in so many words."

She took my hand and I let her. The trains clanged from across the river. I think it was the noise they made when two cars were being fastened together. It must take huge strength to be a trainman, I thought. And you sure wouldn't want to get a hand caught between two of the cars as they banged together.

"Go ahead, Benoit." Helen removed her cold hand from mine.

"Jackson was the only child. His parents tried for another, a brother for Jackson — his maman desired another boy — but she had mis…"

"Miscarriage," said Helen.

"Yes, miscarriage. She had many of those and her doctor said to her, no more. So they decided to adopt. Girl babies were easy to get, but Jackson's mother would not have a girl."

"Why not?" I asked.

Helen put her cold hand on my arm and I bit my tongue.

"I do not know, Violet," said Benoit. "Mrs. Shirt is not a normal person. Many years ago I am sure she is beautiful and kind the way Jackson describes, but crazy does not come in one day. Who knows why she wants another boy baby? Not me."

"Okay, sorry, Benoit, go ahead."

"I should tell the whole story as I know it and then you ask your questions," Benoit said. "It will save a lot of words."

"Okay."

"I tell you, there is much I do not know."

"Just go on," said Helen.

"Okay. So the wait for a boy was long, too long for Madame Shirt, so she went to the underground and found someone who would get her a boy, however grand the cost."

"Oh, dear God," said Helen and picked up the picture of Bertram Shirt.

"This was, uh, eleven years ago," said Benoit.

Helen looked at me. I still didn't get it.

"So these underground men were worse than even Evelyn Shirt understood. She thought she was paying very much money for a baby from a house for not married mothers — not in the law, but with the blessing of the baby's maman. But the man she hired put the money in his pocket and stole babies right out from under the noses of parents or sisters or nannies or who. He even took them from hospital wards. Madame Shirt did not know this. She paid enough to not know."

A trickle of cold sweat ran down my sides and gathered at the waistband of my slacks.

Helen passed me the photograph.

"Bertram isn't a girl," I said. I kept up my struggle against the truth, against the strange recognition that I had sensed the first time I saw the picture. It wasn't Jackson that Bertram resembled, it was my dad, in the pictures I'd seen of him as a boy.

"Bertram is a girl and her name is not Bertram. It is Beatrice," said Benoit. "This is not a good part of the story. The baby-taker grabbed what he thought was a boy and by the time he knew different it was too late. He had a woman with him who cared for the baby on the return to Montreal. She did not know the importance of the sex to the future maman. She cooed its name, "Sunny," which was what the thief heard the baby called by its maman and older sister. I guess by you, Violet. He heard it as "Sonny," and thinks the baby is a boy."

"Wait," I said. I got up and lurched toward some wild yarrow growing in a corner of the yard. I threw up my supper and what felt like part of my innards.

Helen and Benoit sat quietly till I returned to the small circle we made around the photograph.

"Okay", Benoit said, "remember now, that all information I have is third-hand from Jackson, so some could be wrong or not quite right."

"Go on," Helen said.

"Is she still alive?" I asked.

"Yes," said Benoit.

Helen and I looked at each other.

"Benoit, you've got to come back to the house with us and tell it all to Will, before you go any further," said Helen.

"I know I do," he said.

"Why is she all got up like a boy in the picture?" I asked. "Why is Bertram written on the picture? Jackson didn't say anything. We talked about Bertram."

"You surprised him, Violet. He was not ready yet to explain, so he agreed with Beatrice being Bertram."

"Why was she dressed as a boy?" I asked again.

"It was, what you call, a masquerade party. Beatrice dressed as a boy and someone took a picture."

"And labelled it *Bertram*," I said, "and put the name in quotation marks."

"It was the only picture Jackson could find of his sister to bring with him. She was not in many photographs."

"His sister."

"Yes. His sister."

"How did they get away?" I asked. "The people who stole her." I remembered so vividly the search, the lengths that people went to, Ennis Foote's promise to my dad.

"This, I do not know," said Benoit.

"Okay. So Mrs. Shirt didn't want the baby when she saw it was a girl," he went on. "But she was stuck with it."

Helen groaned.

"Her," I said.

"What?"

"Stuck with her. Sunny is a her."

"Yes, pardon me, Violet. So the way Jackson says it, Madame Shirt has not been a good mother to Sunny. That is the worst part of the story."

"Dear God," said Helen.

"Jackson was only six when Beatrice arrived," Benny went on, "too young to question what his mother was or was not doing. But as years passed he did question and object, when he watched her ignore his sister and when he heard Beatrice cry in the night."

"What about the dad?" I asked. "Did he ignore her too?"

"No," Benoit said. "He was a good papa, so Jackson says, tried his best. But he was a busy man with the railroad. And now, of course, he is dead. It is my belief that Papa Shirt's death caused within Jackson the thoughts of finding Beatrice's family. Her true family. His worries about her grew after his papa died."

"Oh, my dear Lord," said Helen. "We've got to go back to the house before you go any further."

The three of us stood up and brushed the dirt from our clothes.

"It is important you know that Jackson came here to try to put this right," said Benny. "He just was not sure how."

"He was certainly taking his time," said Helen.

"Did you know him in Montreal?" I asked.

"No," said Benny. "It is what we said. We met on the road, near Sudbury. There was a camp there, where we both spent a few nights. That is where we heard about the sugar beets."

"So him going out to hoe sugar beets…"

"That was all true," Benny said. "He was going west. And he would stop and see you on the way — make it clean with you folks and leave it to you what you wanted to do."

"Who looked after her," I asked, "if Mrs. Shirt ignored her?"

"Jackson," said Benoit. "Mr. Shirt, as I said, nannies, Mrs. Dunning. Thank God they were rich."

"If they hadn't been rich they wouldn't have had the money to buy her." Helen spat it out.

We trudged down Highfield Street towards home.

"How did Jackson find out who and where we were?" I asked.

"I do not know," said Benoit. "You must save most of your questions for him."

"If he ever turns up," I said. "What if he doesn't turn up?'

"He will."

We turned the corner onto Ferndale and Benny slowed down.

"Jackson was scared," he said.

"He sure didn't seem scared of anything," I said.

"No," said Helen. "He has a very unscared way about him."

"Especially when he found out that Mrs. Palmer had taken her own life," said Benoit. "He got much more afraid then."

I remembered how pale and wobbly he'd gotten when I told him about my mum.

"It has been so much in my head that I can barely believe that not one of you suspected us of anything," said Benoit and stopped walking.

"No," said Helen. "We none of us suspected. Now, Benoit, don't go mentioning worst parts to Will — what you consider to be the worst parts, that type of thing. He is bound to have a differing opinion on that. Come along, now."

And we walked past the last couple of houses to our quiet home and the unsuspecting man inside it.

We found my dad on the verandah.

"Hello," he said. "Benoit, I hear the work is going well on Crawford. Violet, your young friend Isabelle dropped by. She seems anxious to talk to you; she thinks she may have seen Tippy."

Helen herded him into the living room where we all sat down.

"What is it?" he asked. "What's going on? Violet? Are you all right?"

Helen went to make coffee.

Benoit told the story again up to where he had left off with Helen and me, the part where Jackson began to object to the way Beatrice/Sunny was being treated and to worry about her sadness, the part where his dad died.

My dad was shaking. He asked Helen to pour some whiskey into his coffee. She gave us all a little, me less than everybody else.

"You need some food in your stomach," she said to me.

My dad looked grey.

"What was Jackson planning on doing?" he asked. "Where is he?" He stood up.

"I am not certain," said Benoit. "I know he wanted to find you and tell you. He is very worried about Beatrice, uh, Sunny. I do not think he had figured it further because then you folks would be the bosses and it would no longer be up to him alone.

"And, sir, we do not know where he is. He is gone. Disappeared. Without his things."

My dad slammed his glass on the table. "Why, in God's name, had he not said anything to us by now? Why didn't you make him, Benoit?"

"This isn't Benny's fault," I said.

"Of course not. Sorry, Benoit. Who else knows about this? Who all knows?"

"Jackson, me, Tag, you folks. That is all as far as I know," said Benoit. "But I only speak for myself."

And Isabelle in a way and probably the Willis twins and Dirk Botham and maybe Gert Walker, I thought, but kept that information to myself.

"Tag. Why does Tag know?" my dad asked.

"I am sorry, sir. Because I told him. We spent much time together on the road and on the trains. We talked about many things. There were not many topics did not arise."

My dad stood up abruptly. I've got to go to Montreal," he said. "I've got to go now. I'm going down to the train station to get a ticket."

No one slept much. When Helen nagged at Dad to go to bed he said he'd sleep on the train. He drank more whiskey. That scared me a little; it was unlike him and I didn't want him changed in any way.

I dreamed of a man in a tan suit. When I awoke and went back to sleep the man in my dream multiplied and fell apart and turned into a pile of tattered clothes, sticky with blood. Tippy's sweet dead snout poked out from beneath them.

My dad was on a train to Montreal the next day. I swear if there hadn't been a passenger train going he would have hopped a freight along with the hoboes. He had decided to do it on his own, without any help from the police, in the hope that he could. If he couldn't, well, he would cross that bridge when he got to it, he said.

Helen and I wanted him to take Mr. Foote with him, but he balked at the suggestion. I think he was afraid of the hoopla that might occur if word got out, harkening back to that terrible summer of 1925.

"You two keep this under your hats, now," he said when we kissed him goodbye at the station.

As soon as we got home I went over to see Fraser and put him in the picture. He talked me into telling his dad. They promised it would go no further. Mr. Foote wanted to follow my dad to Montreal but he finally agreed to take a wait-and-see approach.

Meanwhile, there was no sign of Jackson.

There was no reason why his vanishing should be associated with the disappearance of our Sunny eleven years ago, and our discovery of his ties to her, but it was connected in all our brains and in my head at least, it stirred up an unholy turmoil.

CHAPTER 27

It was two days later that we read the first report in the paper about the man who had been killed by the railroad tracks. "Vagrant Found Murdered" was the small headline.

Jackson still hadn't turned up. None of us spoke his name but I was certain it was him. So was Helen. Benoit wouldn't believe it.

Any talk about the killing hinted at the involvement of the railroad bulls. From all across the country stories rode in on the rails along with the men about the savage violence of some of those police. They were said to think nothing of bludgeoning vagrants to within inches of their lives. And sometimes the line was crossed. I'd heard it from Isabelle and I'd heard it from Hedley Larkin, both good sources.

The man's name was not released at first because his next of kin had to be notified. A couple of days later he was identified as Jackson Shirde, seventeen, from Montreal. Shirde?

At first all that went on in my brain was *no*. It couldn't be. It couldn't have happened without my seeing him again. I had to go back in time to before he died so I could at least say goodbye. I put on my sneakers and ran, only as far as the river.

Then I couldn't think at all. It was just pictures: Sunny's carriage, a tall man in a tan suit whom I'd never seen before, Margie Willis's grandfather's dirty toes, the boxcar the community club had hauled over to our skating rink last winter as a shelter from the cold (I liked that one), Warren's glowing little face (I liked that one too, but nothing stayed long enough for me to hold onto it). I shivered like my dad did when he found out about Beatrice/Sunny. I noticed that, as if I were observing my own reactions for scientific reasons. It wasn't totally unpleasant.

Jackson had been dead for at least three days. I had laughed on some of those days. Not a lot, though. There hadn't been much to laugh about lately. There had been brief moments of nervous excitement over the idea of Sunny coming home but mostly it was a peaky sort of anticipation. I couldn't picture it at all. I had stolen the photograph of "Bertram" from Jackson's knapsack but couldn't bring myself to look at it again. It rested at the bottom of my underwear drawer, waiting, like I was, for her to come home.

Shirde was Jackson's real last name. Or maybe it wasn't him that the paper had identified; I thought that again and again. But I knew it was. I thought about my dad in Montreal. He was looking for a family of Shirts. I remembered him on the phone with Mrs. Dunning, saying, "Mrs. Shirt." She would have been saying, "Mrs. Shirde." But over the phone lines I supposed they sounded very much alike.

When I went back to the house Helen was on the phone to my dad at his hotel in Montreal saying, "Shirde," spelling it out for him: "S H I R D E." She didn't tell him how she knew; she didn't mention Jackson's death. I suppose she didn't want him to feel worse about taking Mrs. Shirde's remaining child. Helen's face was a crumpled mess. She pulled herself together for the duration of the telephone conversation.

I walked over to see Benny. He was sitting alone in a corner of the yard. It was obvious to me that he had heard. When I came near him his eyes were flat at first but he seemed to quickly click into my presence from wherever he had been.

"How does that help?" I asked.

"What?" Benny said.

"Your stupid trances. How do they help?"

"Help what?" Benny asked.

"Anything," I said. "What's the point?" Then I burst into tears and Benny leapt up and wound his skinny arms around me. I sobbed noisily into his sleeve while several builders looked on.

"Did you know his name wasn't even Shirt?" I asked.

"No," said Benny and smoothed the hair away from my face. "No, I did not know that. Perhaps he changed his name for the trip west."

Benny needed to get back to work, so I left him and roamed the streets. I tried to convince myself that there were two rambling seventeen-year-old Jacksons from Montreal with similar last names, neither of which I'd heard before. And my Jackson was still alive.

I went home to Helen. She didn't talk to me much in those first days after Jackson's death. She didn't talk a whole lot to anyone. Mrs. Foote came over, but she wanted to pray with us and neither Helen nor I would have it.

Helen's only words could have been spoken by anyone: "supper's ready," "don't forget your satchel," "how were classes today?" She wasn't unpleasant, but I knew she didn't care about answers. I grew uncomfortable around her, more so than when Jackson was a living being between us. Her sorrow, her mourning, seemed to take on a certain aggression — like a renunciation of sorts — of hope? of visions of rapture? — I couldn't know. Whatever it was, it shut me out. I wanted what now seemed impossible — to rest my head against her shoulder with both her arms around me for a long, long time. I felt like I needed more comfort than I was getting and that caused me to want to bonk her on the head with the cast-iron frying pan.

Dusty gauze cloaked the first couple of days and whetted blades lurked beneath it, never buried deep enough for safety or comfort. I couldn't wash myself and I had trouble swallowing anything, even my own spit. It seemed like the last time I was able to take a deep breath was the night I got drunk. My whole body ached from trying. Also, I had to get away from Helen, but I didn't want to be alone.

I went with Gwen to visit Warren.

"Tag's dead, isn't he?" Warren said.

"What?" I said.

"Tag's dead."

"Well, no, not that we know of," I said. "Why do you say that?"

"We heard Nurse Parnell talking to Nurse Miles about a dead Negro, killed by the railroad tracks. Tag's the only Negro around. I don't like Nurse Parnell. She's the only one here that isn't nice. She said 'nigger' like mum does."

"This is news to us, Warren, but we'll find out," Gwen said and she marched out of the ward to the nurse's station.

"The way we heard it was that Jackson died," I said to Warren.

I knew it didn't work to keep secrets that big. He would find out in the wind or from Nurse Parnell and then he would blame us for not coming clean.

"Jackson?"

"Yeah," I said.

"Is this to do with your sister, Violet?" Warren asked.

My temples squeezed inwards till I had to close my eyes and hold my head.

"What are you talking about, Warren?" I asked.

"Tag told me about your baby sister," he said.

Robert walked slowly over from his bed to join us and Gwen came back at the same time.

"Hi, Robert," Gwen said.

"Hi, Gwen," he said. "Hi, Violet."

"What gives?" said Warren. "Who's dead and who isn't?"

"Nurse Parnell's not on duty but Nurse Miles said that Nurse Parnell's brother is a cop and that he said that the man who was found by the tracks was a Negro."

I sat down in a metal chair and put my head between my knees, something Helen had taught me. My dizziness passed and after a few moments I sat up.

"Are you okay, Violet?" asked Warren.

"Yes, I think so," I said.

Gwen went into Warren's tiny washroom and came back with a cold cloth that she pressed against my forehead.

"So, are Jackson and Tag both dead?" I asked, still reeling from what Warren had said about Sunny. Did everyone in the world know way more than I did about me and my very own family? "Or is Jackson still alive or what? Jesus!"

"I don't know," said Gwen, "but I told Nurse Miles to tell Nurse Parnell to watch her tongue around young boys."

"We're not young boys," said Warren. He included Robert in his statement.

"What are you?" I asked, trying to act normal.

"I don't know, middle-age boys, I guess. We're not young."

We promised him we would find out what was what.

"Please find out it wasn't Tag," said Warren. "Or Jackson, either. I like him, too. Why does it have to be either of them?"

"Maybe it isn't," said Gwen. "Maybe it's neither and it's all a big mistake."

I think we all doubted that.

We were both quiet on the way home. I hadn't told Gwen anything about finding Sunny. I didn't want her mum knowing any more of our business than she already did, shadowing it as she had with her dark thoughts. But Warren knew about my long-lost sister!

"Has your mum been to see Warren?" I asked, now dreading any contact between the two in case Warren spilled the beans. I needed to speak to him again.

"No," said Gwen.

"What does your brother know about Sunny?' I asked.

"Who?"

"My sister," I said.

"Nothing," said Gwen. "Not that I know of. Why?"

So Gwen wasn't in the picture. I believed that.

"I don't want Tag to be dead," I said. Maybe even more than I didn't want Jackson to be dead, I realized, and then understood there had been a small amount of relief attached to Jackson's death.

"No," Gwen said. "We've got to find out what's going on. Maybe you could ask Frank's dad?"

"Yeah."

We walked along Bartlet Avenue in silence for a while. The street was empty except for an Eaton's delivery wagon and a '33 Plymouth parked on the road. And the tail end of a young boy on his bicycle turning the corner onto Osborne Street. A dog trotted along at his side.

"Any sign of Tippy?" I asked.

"No," said Gwen.

I remembered Isabelle then and her possible sighting of the dog, but I didn't mention it. I didn't want to get Gwen's hopes up. Maybe I could see Isabelle today sometime.

We leaned into the thin fall air; it was an effort for me to move forward. And in this pale new world of death and loss and middle-age boys, even the chrysanthemums and asters looked dull. I could barely see them.

"Did your mum ever hear back from Mr. Roosevelt about going to that polio place?" I asked.

"No, but Eleanor Roosevelt wrote Warren a letter wishing him well."

It became, not easy, but not difficult, either, to keep certain feelings at bay. Whenever they began to creep in, I recognized them as something to be put aside, dealt with later.

I didn't feel like talking to Mr. Foote. I went to see Isabelle instead. She was babysitting, but we went outside and sat on the steps of her apartment building.

She was matter-of-fact about Jackson's death. She had heard about it, although not from the newspaper.

"I heard people talking about it at Jimmie's," she said.

"Who's Jimmie?"

"It's not a who. It's a what," she said. "A coffee shop downtown. But I heard that the dead man was a Negro," she went on.

"No, I don't think that's right," I said. "It was Jackson. Wasn't it? Could you please find out if two men died?"

I realized I might have to go and see Fraser's dad after all. He would know what was going on.

"The Willis twins and creepy Dirk were at Jimmie's," Isabelle said. "They seemed really interested in the man named Jackson's death."

"Interested like how?" A crawly feeling snaked up and down my sides beneath the sweat.

I could see their ears perking up," Isabelle said.

"What did that look like?"

"They were almost but not quite twitching." Isabelle laughed. She could. This had no real connection to her other than through me. And who the heck was I? A rich girl from The Flats that she probably didn't even like all that much.

"But since then I heard that the man was coloured so I don't even know if it was the same Jackson."

"This is crazy," I said. "Tag's a coloured man, but his name isn't Jackson and we're all hoping he's gone home to Detroit."

I told her the news about Sunny. She took it in stride as she did pretty well everything, but she found it interesting.

"You're going through a hell of a lot right now, aren't you, Vi?" She put her arm around my shoulders.

My eyes burned. "It sure feels like it."

"I'll keep my ear to the ground," she said.

When I stood up to leave she said, "That dog you're looking for? The one I met at Happyland that night?"

"Tippy." I had completely forgotten about her. For a little while, anyway.

"I'm pretty sure I saw her under the bridge," Isabelle said, "and then again behind the hospital at the river. I think she's living semi-wild, with some tramps."

"Thanks, Is."

Briggs Hardware was across the street on Taché. I stopped there and bought a dog collar and a leash. Then I followed the path by the river from north of St. Boniface Hospital, under the bridge, past the rowing club and the motorboat garage all the way to St. Mary's Road.

Some of the scruffy characters I spoke to seemed familiar with Tippy when I described her to them. One young boy tramp who I was sure was a girl knew her quite well, she said, and was glad to find out her name. I gave her my address and the collar and leash and a dollar and asked her to bring Tippy to me if she should see her again. The hobo's name was Bill.

Back home, I told Aunt Helen to expect a young girl hobo pretending to be a boy named Bill to turn up at any time with

Tippy Walker. I didn't have the strength to tell her anything else, especially about the possibility of Tag being dead. There had to be more than one Negro in Winnipeg. I just hoped it wasn't Tag's brother.

CHAPTER 28

Two things happened that crossed each other in time.

When my dad phoned next he told us that he had seen Jackson: that was the first thing.

We told him that Jackson was dead.

He said, "No, he's not." He told us he'd call back after he had spoken to him again.

The second thing was that Jackson's uncle, Bernard Shirde, his dad's brother, came to Winnipeg and confirmed that the dead vagrant was not his nephew. Not even close. And then he went home again; we never got to meet him.

I phoned Frank and asked him to ask his dad some questions.

"Mr. Shirde could have saved himself a trip if someone had mentioned to him that the dead man was a Negro," said Mr. Foote.

My dad phoned back and told Jackson's story to Helen the way it had been told to him. He told it nervously because of the long distance charges. And then Helen told it to me. I hated Jackson's story.

"What about Sunny?" I had asked repeatedly in the background when Helen was on the phone.

"What about Sunny?" she finally said to my dad.

"He has her," she whispered to me after listening for a moment or two.

"Come home, Will," she said next. "Come home as soon as you can."

"What do you mean he has her?" I asked when my aunt finally hung up.

"Your father has Sunny with him. They're coming home," Helen said. "Jackson's mother is still in the rest home."

"What about Mrs. Dunning?" I asked.

"Your dad saw both of them, talked to them both. He'll explain it all to us when he gets home."

"It sounds like no one put up much of a fight to keep Sunny," I said. "Not that I wanted it to be hard for Dad, but…"

"I know what you mean," said Helen. "It's hard to imagine."

My chest hurt and I tried to breathe through the pain. I couldn't get a satisfying breath. "Dad will be really nice to her, won't he, Helen? He'll know what to do? How to be with her?"

"Of course he'll be nice to her, Violet. He's doing the absolute best he can. The best he knows how."

"I wish I'd gone with him," I said, gasping for more air.

"You've got university," said Helen in her new absent way.

I didn't mention that I hadn't been attending. I was always heading out somewhere, so she hadn't noticed or at least hadn't let on.

CHAPTER 29

The papers then reported that the man found dead by the tracks wasn't Jackson Shirde after all. He was a Negro and they didn't know who he was. They revealed that he had been covered with tar and thistles and that the police believed foul play was involved but had arrested no one. He was naked under the tar and his clothes had been found nearby, cut to shreds, with Jackson Shirde's identification in a pocket. Hence, the mix-up. That was all the paper had to say about it other than that he was very thin.

Foul play indeed. Play didn't get much fouler.

It was Tag; I knew it; we all knew it. Benny stepped up to identify him and it was then that one paper reported: The thin Negro has been identified as Taggart Woodman of Detroit, Michigan. Age: eighteen. The other paper didn't bother.

I went over to see Benny the day of the identification. He was still living at the construction site on Crawford.

He told me that Tag's head was gone and that the tar had made a terrible mess of his body. Benny told the officials that he recognized Tag's hands and his overall size. That had been good enough for whoever was in charge.

"They didn't clean him up very well," he said now. "I hate to think of his family seeing him like that."

"Will they be sending him home to Detroit?" I asked, deciding to wait a while, maybe a good long while, before thinking about the state Tag Woodman was in.

"They haven't found his parents yet, but I'm going to pester them till they do. Maybe I'll take him home when they find them. I would talk them into burying him without looking at him."

"That's very kind, Benoit."

He grunted — a French-Canadian grunt.

"They let me sit with him a while," he said. "That is how I knew it was Tag. No one would have been able to know, to…rec…"

"Recognize," I said.

"Yes, to recognize what was left under that sheet, except maybe the boy's mother."

"Oh, Benoit."

"Yes. But he spoke to me, Violet. Not out loud, of course. But Tag spoke to me and he seemed, how do you say? at peace."

I nodded.

"He wasn't angry or hurting. I felt a little sadness from him, maybe, but mostly a quiet peace."

"That's good, Benoit."

"It was Tag all right." He sighed.

"I'm glad you were here to identify him, Benoit, and that he didn't just get lost in a pile of…."

"Dead tramps," said Benny.

"Yes."

"You asked me one day, you said, how do your trances help?"

"Yes?"

"I am not sure how to explain it, Vi. I know I cannot go back through time or anything. But I swear my training put me in touch with Tag there in that cold morgue room. I swear. If I keep at it, something more could happen. And if it does not…well, I liked very much saying goodbye to Tag."

"Why did it happen, Benny?" I asked. "Why would anyone kill him?"

"I do not know, Violet." He sighed again. "Maybe we will never know. Some people do not need a very good reason to kill."

Not good enough, I thought.

Benny told me then that Tag had been a religious man, heavily into everlasting life, Jesus, the whole thing.

"Good," I said. "That probably helped him meet his death."

"Yeah," said Benny. "He was an Episcopalian."

When I left Benoit, I caught a streetcar that would take me to the King George to see Warren. I was mad at that shitheel Jackson for being alive. I looked out the window and tried to decide on the words I would use to tell Warren about Tag. Getting nowhere with that, I realized I would just have to let it happen. Warren would help me. Besides which, he had already told me. He already knew, thanks to that awful Nurse Parnell.

The streets of Winnipeg had changed; it was more than just the autumn light. It's me, I thought; I'm seeing things differently now. Some edges appeared sharper, pitch-dark against the light, others were blurry, like I needed glasses. I could have sworn some things were missing entirely from the landscape while others were brand new, without a speck of dust on them.

Warren had already done his crying, he explained, when he didn't shed a tear.

Robert came to join us but Warren asked him to leave us for a while. We had some private things to talk about.

Jackson had told Benoit, Benoit had told Tag and Tag had told Warren that Jackson's mission while in Winnipeg was to inform the Palmer family that their daughter, Beatrice, was alive and living in Montreal. He wanted to put things right.

But he had struggled. He was afraid of causing trouble for his mother, whom he described as fragile. And there was finding out that my own mother had killed herself after the baby was snatched. That added another layer of horror. Also there was fear of the consequences of his own involvement after all those years of knowing and not speaking up.

It surprised me a little that Tag had confided in Warren. Surely the age difference would have limited the kind of talk that passed between them. It turned out that Warren had heard the three of them talking about the situation: Jackson, Benoit, and Tag. He heard enough that he wanted to know more. He pestered Tag till he told him the whole story, that day I had found them whittling outside Tag's tent.

"Why didn't you tell me, Warren?" I asked now.

"I wasn't supposed to," he said.

How could I blame Warren for anything? It wasn't his fault three grown men were careless enough to get him involved in something so sinister.

"How did Jackson find us?" I asked.

"I don't know," said Warren.

It wouldn't have been hard, I realized. With all the publicity surrounding Sunny's kidnapping a matter of public record, it would be easy enough for a curious teenager to find out what he was looking for.

CHAPTER 30

Jackson came back on the train with my dad and Sunny. Helen drove the Buick to the station where I laid eyes on my sister for the first time in eleven years. There aren't many hallowed moments in one person's life: this was one of mine. She smiled shyly at me and I loved her instantly and completely.

She wore loose comfy trousers and a modern haircut. The word fashionable came to mind. Someone had been taking care of certain of her needs, anyway.

We all went back to the house where Helen and I served tea and tomato sandwiches and angel food cake with butter icing.

Sunny sat close to Jackson and it occurred to me then that I would have him on the edges my life for the long run. This brother and sister were not going to let go of each other. I looked at Helen, wondering if she was realizing the same thing. We were practically related to Jackson. She was brisk and busy, giving nothing away but kindness to Sunny.

Words fell out of Jackson's mouth like miniature dead sparrows and landed on the hardwood floor in front of the chesterfield. Helen's words fared better, but she was trying for Sunny's sake. I don't think I spoke at all and my dad said very little. He was exhausted. He did ask Jackson to tell his story again, which he did.

Jackson had gone looking for Tag and found him at the river, on the other side, below Dominion Envelope and Cartons. They sat and talked and were approached by three men. He recognized Dirk Botham from the W.C. Fields night at the movies. The other two were unfamiliar to him but they looked alike so he assumed they were brothers.

Dirk did the talking. He told Jackson to get lost forever. They forced him to hand over his ID and they put it in Tag's pocket. Tell no one. Leave town. Don't even go back to your camp and get your stuff. They talked about what they would do to Tag: they wouldn't hurt him if Jackson left; they would hurt him very badly if he didn't. They also described what they would do to Benoit and even to Helen and me. Jackson didn't go into detail and we didn't ask. Their scare tactics worked.

Why couldn't Tag just have gone home to Detroit? I wondered. Brother or no brother. I couldn't bear that Jackson had left him with Dirk Botham and the Willises. I hated him for that.

Jackson went on to say that Tag had tried convincing the criminals that he was preparing to leave Winnipeg the very day they had caught up with him. He had found no trace of his brother and the hope of finding him had been the only thing keeping him here. He assured them that if they let him go they would never see him again. His plea fell on deaf ears. Tag encouraged Jackson to leave, told him he'd be all right.

"Both of us knew it wasn't true, but I didn't guess how bad it would be," Jackson said. "Maybe Tag did. So I left him with those men. God help me, I'm ashamed of that," he said. "I'll be ashamed till the day I die." Tears streamed down Jackson's face. He looked like he hadn't slept since he left Tag at the river

Sunny took one of his hands in both of hers.

My dad phoned Mr. Foote and then he and Jackson went down to the police station to see him.

Nothing about Jackson Shirt was extra good. But he wasn't bad either. He was just a boy. And he did bring Sunny back to us. That was as good as good could get.

Helen and I took Sunny and her small suitcase up to the spare room, which was no longer spare. It was Sunny's and we had painted it a pale yellow while we waited for her to come home.

"I'll rest till Jackson comes back," she said. Her voice was so sweet I wanted to swallow it.

When Helen asked her what she would like to be called she said, "Sunny, please. I like the name Sunny."

Helen showed her the bathtub and we let her be.

We took cups of tea out to the verandah, where we sat in silence.

A few minutes later, Bill, the girl hobo, trotted up the street towards us with Tippy at the end of a leash.

"Oh, thank God," I said and ran out to meet them.

Tippy squealed and jumped up on me.

"You crazy girl," I said. "If you're so happy to see me, why didn't you just come over here in the first place?"

Helen gave Bill food and drink and a small amount of cash. She offered her a bath, too, but the girl said no and went on her way.

Dirk Botham was soon rounded up and he was quick to finger the Willis twins and Gert Walker, too, who he insisted put them up to it. She was as guilty as any tar-wielding teenager. I wanted everyone but Warren to know that. She blamed our family and our strange men for Warren's polio. Specifically, she blamed Tag. I witnessed her reaction that day in her kitchen when she saw her little boy frolicking in the field with the coloured man. In her mind he may as well have injected Warren with a syringe full of the paralyzing disease.

There was no logic, but she didn't need any. She just needed someone to blame. So she and Dirk Botham gunned for Tag and they enlisted the dirty Willis brothers to help them.

But there was a connection to Sunny. A contorted, misinformed, unseeing connection that Isabelle discovered at Jimmie's Coffee Shop. She overheard part of a conversation between the Willis twins. She reported it to me and I passed it on to my dad and Mr. Foote and it was folded into the admixture of evil.

One of the Willises had eavesdropped on Tag and Warren one day as they sat together in Tag's camp. He hid behind a bush just for the heck of it and listened in. Tag had been talking about Jackson's mission to tell us about Sunny.

Those good words, those brave words, those right-thing-to-do words entered that Willis head and sat there a while, changing shape a little. By the time they made their way to the other Willis they held little resemblance to their original form. They were all wrong.

The twins remembered that time long ago when they had helped search for a stolen baby. They hadn't forgotten that reward money. Maybe there was still a chance for them to claim it. When they were finished with their talk, Tag was the kidnapper and it was their job to put him to rights. Never mind Gert's theory that he had given Warren polio. They didn't get that he would have been five years old at the time of Sunny's disappearance. A fact like that wasn't applicable in the Willis world.

"Well, someone to do with him then," Lump Willis cried out in court. "If it wasn't him it musta been someone to do with the nigra."

CHAPTER 31

So there we sat, Fraser and me, with Johnny Lee at his dining room table in Riverview. It was three months, nearly to the day, since Jackson and Benoit had first walked into our back yard.

"The man was a Negro," Johnny said now.

"Yes," said I.

Johnny blew his nose in Fraser's handkerchief.

"One of his hands stuck out of the thistles right next to the rail," he said. "That's how we decided that he was a coloured man. We still weren't sure, though. Artie thought he mighta just turned dark because he was dead. I don't know very much about dead people yet. He was my first one ever. Artie saw his grandmother after she died, but she was in a coffin and all fixed up for the viewing. There weren't any flies or missing pieces. He said she looked pretty white to him. Whiter than usual even."

"Is there anything else, Johnny?" I asked after a full minute went by. "Anything at all you'd like to tell us?"

"No."

"Would you be willing to take us there?" I asked.

"Violet, I don't think…" Fraser began.

"I can't leave my sister and it's too far to take her," Johnny said.

"Of course," I said. What did I know about younger sisters? My lack of knowledge about the topic could have filled several boxcars.

"I could draw you a map," he said.

"Great idea!"

He tried to hand the soaked handkerchief back to Fraser.

"Keep it," Fraser said.

Johnny got a piece of paper and a pencil from the kitchen and with his lips pressed together in a taut thin line he drew a clear and complete map of the area, including approximate distances. He even added a few trees and a square box that represented the J.S. Coal Company. It was just north of the coal company that they had found Tag.

"This is fantastic," I said. I dug in the pocket of my skirt for my change purse and pulled out a dollar bill.

Johnny's mouth opened and shut, opened and shut.

"The Negro's thumb had come away from his hand," he said. "I think the train did it, but neatly, not like with his head. The thumb was lying on its own just inside the rail."

Apparently, I had bought myself more information.

"Artie picked it up. I told him to leave it but he wouldn't. He put in his pocket. He said no one would miss it."

Fraser and I exchanged a look. Artie was probably right.

"That's when I threw my wiener away, I think," Johnny said. "And then I threw up."

"So Artie kept the thumb?" I asked. "He took it home with him?"

"Yup," said Johnny. "He sure did. We went up to the fire station to tell what we saw and the whole time we were talkin' to the firemen Artie had the dead man's thumb in his pocket."

"Holy doodle," I said.

"Yup," he said.

We got a tiny smile out of him then, the only one we saw.

Johnny saw us to the back door. I felt bad leaving him, but I was pretty sure he felt okay about talking to us.

"Promise you won't tell the part about Artie taking the man's thumb," he said through the screen door.

"Cross my heart and hope to die," I said, going through the actions. It was the least I could do.

"Okay."

"Thanks, Johnny."

His sister, Muriel, was in the sandbox with a friend, making what looked to be sand cakes and cookies and setting them on a sand table for them to pretend to eat.

"'Bye, Muriel," I said and gave a small wave as we headed towards the back gate.

"I love the baby Jesus and she loves me," she called after us.

"Me too," shouted her friend who was even smaller than she was.

"I think Jesus was a boy," I called back.

They looked at me in stunned surprise.

All the stuff I could have taught Sunny through the years, all the things she could have taught me, made me dizzy. I tried to look forward to what was still ahead for us. Looking back at all that could have been was much too sad, especially the fragile shadow that was my mother. If only she could have been here for Sunny's return.

Fraser and I walked down Osborne Street past the St. Mary's Cemetery toward downtown. Following the directions on Johnny's map, we turned right on Mulvey Avenue East and as soon as we could we climbed up onto the tracks. We walked along on the wooden slats, the spaces between them not quite wide enough for a grown-up's stride. It would have been just right for two eleven-year-olds.

There were no police markers or anything at all to distinguish the area where Tag had been placed to die. But I'm pretty sure it would have found me even if we hadn't had Johnny's good map. Maybe Benny was rubbing off on me. A funny thing happened: it started out slow at first, a buzzing sound in my head and a dizziness that brought me to my knees without my realizing it.

"Are you okay, Violet?" Fraser asked.

The sound grew louder and higher pitched. It was like strange voices in a faraway marketplace with the clatter and noise of life filling in the spaces around them. It rose and fell, filling my head, then withdrawing with an abruptness that made me look around for it, as though it were something that could be seen.

"I think this is it," I said. "This is the spot."

Fraser looked at the map and identified a dead tree that Johnny had pencilled in. He had described it as "the hanging tree."

"I think you're right," he said. "Come away, Violet, let's sit over here on this pile of dirt."

There was nothing left there to describe what had happened to Tag. I stood up and poked my foot around in the gravel and dirt but nothing leapt out at me. I don't know what I was looking for.

The wind came up and blew dirt into our faces.

"Let's just go, Fraser," I said.

We stumbled back through the CN yards till we got to Osborne. The Rome Café was on the other side of the street so we crossed over and stopped in for a drink. I had coffee and Fraser had tea. We were the only customers.

"Nasty business, that," said the man behind the counter and gestured with his head toward the other side of the street. I guess he had watched us come up from the river.

Neither of us answered. My coffee tasted like slop.

We took a streetcar home; we were both too exhausted to walk.

That night Fraser got hold of some lemon gin and I got drunk for the second time in my life. We mixed it with ginger ale and drank the whole mickey between us down by the river, across from the icehouse. It was pleasant; the gin made me fuzzy and dull, which was exactly what I wanted. Fraser walked me home at midnight and kissed me on the lips.

CHAPTER 32

I went to visit Warren on a late October morning when only the most stubborn of leaves remained clinging to their black branches. It was my least favourite time of year, dismal and grey, with thoughts of winter on everyone's mind. If last winter was anything to go by, we were in for a deep dark freeze. A low feeling always came over me in the autumn of the year, but not this low. I shivered in my fall coat and welcomed the warm air of the hospital lobby.

Warren was sitting up on the side of his bed smiling from ear to ear. A young orderly was detaching a brace from his weak leg. Some of the feeling had come back to it.

"Hi, Violet!" he said. "I've decided what I'm going to be when I grow up."

The orderly smiled at me as he stowed the brace away in a cupboard by the bed.

"Do you want to stay sitting up, Sport?" he asked Warren.

"Yes, please, Martin, for a while, anyway."

Martin adjusted some pillows behind Warren and helped him to arrange his legs under a sheet.

"So what are you gonna be when you grow up?" I asked when the orderly was gone.

"A brace maker," said Warren. "They're called calipers sometimes and that's what I'm going to call them. The name of my company is going to be Comfy Calipers. See, this one that I've been using is horrible." He pointed to the cupboard. "It rubs in all the wrong places and hurts. So I'm gonna redesign it till it feels good, till it feels like I'm wearing nothing at all and then I'm going to sell it to the world and become rich and maybe even famous."

"Sounds good," I said, and sat down in the straight-backed chair next to the bed.

"Where's Gwen?" he asked. He no longer mentioned his mum.

"She got a job," I said. "That's my big news. She got a job at Eaton's mail order, so between the two of you, you'll be fabulously wealthy in no time."

"I think it may take me a little while to get my project off the ground." Warren grinned. "I thought they turned Gwen down again."

"They did, but they got back in touch yesterday and she's hired on as of this morning."

"Great!"

"Yeah, it is great," I said.

I reached in my bag and pulled out a Tootsie Roll, a drawing pad and some pencils of different widths sharpened to fine points. "These are for you to mess around with," I said.

Warren's eyes got big. "This is terrific, Violet. I can draw calipers."

"You can draw whatever you want," I said and looked around. "Where's Robert?"

"He's gone home."

"That's wonderful," I said.

"Yeah, but I miss him." He started unwrapping the Tootsie Roll.

"Still."

"Yeah."

There was a small boy on a rocking bed and an even smaller boy attached to a Bradford frame. His head looked too big for his body.

"I can talk to them when Martin helps me get up and around," said Warren, nodding toward his two roommates. "I've been getting quite a bit more exercise now that I have more feeling in my leg."

"Things are going well, aren't they, Warren?"

He was beginning to slump slightly against his pillows with his treat still unbitten, so I helped him lie down and started toward the door to let him rest.

"Why did Tag have to die, Violet?" he asked.

I came back to the side of his bed.

"That's a tough question, Warren, and I'm afraid I don't know the answer to it. Not any answer that makes sense, anyway."

"I heard they caught the guys who did it."

"Yeah."

I wondered if Warren knew about his mother's involvement.

"It was the Willis twins," I said.

"And Dirk," said Warren.

"Yeah, he was more like the foreman. He gave the orders and the Willis boys did the work."

"I knew he was bad."

"Yeah. I know you did."

"What will happen to them?"

"I don't know. They're all in jail now, I know that much. But they have yet to come to trial."

"How could Gwen have been so stupid as to like him?" Warren asked.

"I don't know, Warren. Sometimes even smart people do stupid things. She sure doesn't like him anymore."

"Did Tag's brother Duke ever turn up?" Warren asked.

"He's back in Detroit," I said. "And Benoit took Tag home to his folks there as well."

"That's good," Warren said.

"Tag was an Episcopalian," I said.

"What's that?"

"I'm not sure. I think it sits somewhere between a Catholic and a Protestant."

When I thought Warren had drifted off, I began to leave again.

"Let's build a monument," he said.

I turned back. "Yes, let's."

"For Tag," he said. And then I was sure he was asleep.

And he was going to be able to walk.

I stopped at the motorboat launch on my way home, sat on the wooden dock and thought carefully for a long, long time. It was mid-afternoon, not a bad time of day. I couldn't remember ever feeling so sad and so happy all at the same time. My breaths came easily and I savoured the feeling that I was getting enough air to survive, to thrive even.

My schoolwork had gotten away on me. I was already so far behind that I had decided to quit and take the year off. When I told my dad, he didn't object, and Helen was glad. It was my job, and hers, to help Sunny learn to live inside a new family and I needed to be around.

AFTERWORD

With Dirk and the Willis twins and Gert Walker all blaming each other, and the train doing the actual killing, it was difficult to sort things out clearly in court. But they all spent time behind bars.

Dirk went to the Headingly Correctional Institution just west of Winnipeg, where he spent just three years. The Botham family moved away from the province of Manitoba. The speculation was that they wished to avoid humiliation and receive Dirk on his release and offer him a new start where the family was not known.

The Willis boys went to Stony Mountain Penitentiary. Their previous records hurt them and they both ended up dying in jail, one from tuberculosis and one from having his throat slit, ear to ear.

And Gert went to the new Prison for Women in Kingston, Ontario. She wasn't able to weasel her way out of a prison sentence. So she lost her cleaning jobs and her little house on Lawndale Avenue. She'd already lost her kids. She was probably out of prison in just a few years; I can picture her tricking people into thinking she was behaving well. But she never reappeared in Winnipeg as far as I know. For a while I pictured her as a scrubwoman in a bleak industrial town in the east. And then I stopped picturing her at all.

Two surprising things came out in the courtroom. One was that the old man at the Willis place, long dead now — the man I'd seen cutting his toenails — was the twins' father as well as their grandfather. Their mother, therefore, was also their sister. That really threw people for a loop.

The second surprising thing was that Gwen's mother, Gert, turned out to be Galechka Wynchenko, a Ukrainian girl from across the tracks in the North End. And all her talk of garlic eaters and bohunks! I guess she was ashamed of her beginnings, as so many are, and was never who she said she was.

Not even Gwen knew.

"You'd think she could have picked a better name than Gert," I said to her, after she had stopped being completely stunned.

"She could have told me," Gwen said. "I wish she would have told me."

I don't know how much Gwen revealed to Warren at the time. She made me promise to leave it up to her and not go blurting things out to him. Eventually, I'm sure he heard all of it. He wasn't the type of boy you held things back from.

Gwen and Mary became good friends; they worked in the same office at Eaton's. They rented a big beautiful suite together on the first floor of the Ladywood Block on Edmonton Street. Warren went to live with them there and enrolled after Christmas at Isbister School on Vaughan Street. Tippy joined them in their new home after several weeks at our house. By the following summer Warren walked with a barely discernible limp. And by the time he was in high school he was going by the name of Warren Wynchenko. Comfy Calipers fell by the wayside; Warren went on to become a builder of houses.

The man who kidnapped Sunny was never found. And we never discovered how he got away. Jackson's dad had not been involved at all. It was Evelyn Shirde who hired the man to find her a baby. My memory, if that's what it was, of the man in the tan suit, was no more helpful today than someone else's memory of him had been eleven years before. I mentioned it to Mr. Foote anyway. He was so happy for us, but he berated himself for the rest of his life for not trying harder to find our girl.

Mrs. Shirde was judged to be incompetent, needing round-the-clock professional care, and was to be institutionalized for the rest of her life.

Jackson would stay in touch with Sunny over the years, so to me he became like a half-brother once-removed or something at least as confusing. There was no real name for what we were to each other. It was strange at first, having loved him the way I had. Those kinds of feelings had no place in the new life. It was necessary to begin again with him in a completely different way.

We never saw Benoit again, after he left on the train to take Tag home. Whether he finally slipped through a fissure or simply went back to Montreal, I don't know.

My dad went back to work at his law office in the fall and put off painting the garage till the spring of '37. He asked Hedley Larkin to give him a hand and they finally got the job done.

Helen worried me. That summer left her different. It was as though something had been stolen from her, something irreplaceable. Sunny's sweet new presence went a long way, but there was something sucked out of Helen that never returned. The person I had always looked to for comfort was still there, but I had to search for her anew each time I needed her. Maybe it was someone else's turn now. I think some people allow themselves to be squeezed dry by those around them and they have to change into someone else in order to continue on. This may be what happened to Helen. And I was one of the ones who squeezed her.

As I came to see her more clearly, I knew that in my own mind I had skewed her feelings for Jackson. Maybe I hadn't exaggerated the strength of her love, but I'd skewed it, drastically.

Sunny never cut her hair after she came to live with us, except to trim the ends. She struggled and she wept for the mother she left in Montreal. But she also laughed and grew strong and pursued a career in nursing, like Aunt Helen. And she has never strayed far from her home. Sunny is a rare beauty; she looks like our mother.

Eventually I returned to college where I took my arts degree, but I never could decide on a career. Motherhood took care of that and my regrets rear up just occasionally. Fraser Foote became a policeman like his dad and I became Fraser's wife. It's 1960 as I write these last words and we are the proud parents of a fine son named Frank. I worried when he was young that he would be snatched away from me as Sunny had been, but Fraser has helped me not to smother him.

Jackson Shirt — I could never get used to Shirde — returned to Montreal but we continue to see him now and then when he comes to visit Sunny. I still like to think that he never kissed me because he thought of me as a sort of half-sister. Looking at him as time passes I struggle to find the boy I loved so much inside the man's portly frame. I prefer to close my eyes and conjure up that summer of '36. I hang on to it like it was a golden time, like it was really something.